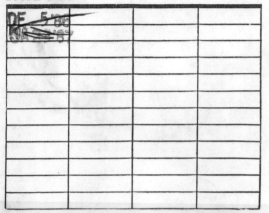

Love
in
All Its
Disguises

BY NORMAN ROSTEN

Novels
Under the Boardwalk
Over and Out
Love in All Its Disguises

Poetry
Return Again, Traveler
The Fourth Decade
The Big Road
Songs for Patricia
The Plane and the Shadow
Thrive Upon the Rock
Selected Poems

Plays
Mister Johnson
Come Slowly, Eden

Memoir
Marilyn: An Untold Story

Love in All Its Disguises

A Novel by

Norman Rosten

ARBOR HOUSE
New York

Library of Congress Catalog Card Number: 81-065135

ISBN: 0-87795-324-4

Manufactured in the United States of America

10   9   8   7   6   5   4   3   2   1

For Patricia

Cant we stay out just a little while longer?
Your watch is fast, papa—don't you remember?
Who wants to go home on a night like this?
We can always go home,—down to that old
charnel house in the valley. We ask you,
when will another carnival come
to this godforsaken place? This is the first
and it will probably be the last.
O flesh, farewell!

—Ettore Rella

I.

1.

Donald reached for the phone at the end of its first ring, at the same time his eye caught the clock on the small night-table. Morning light helped him to see the dial face: six-thirty. He turned his head into the pillow, away from the sleeping figure beside him. Who could it be? A nervous client? It wasn't a court day, he knew that instinctively. Or his son calling from college? But if Andy needed money, the kid was smart enough to know he'd have a better chance by asking at a more reasonable hour.

"Yes?" he asked, cupping the phone. "Who is it?"

"Donnie?" One word, high, tight, at the edge of a scream. He recognized it at once, although it was months since she last called.

"Yes, Fran. What's the matter?"

"Momma . . ." The voice stopped, seemed to take a breath.

"What is it?"

"Momma's dead." The phone clicked off.

"Hello. Fran?" He jiggled the receiver. Silence. The operator was unable to trace the call, it was made from an outdoor booth. And he couldn't call back later since she had moved recently and as usual kept it secret.

He heard his wife mumble drowsily, "What is it, dear?"
"Nothing, Debbie. Go back to sleep. Call you later."

He slipped out of bed, closed the door behind him and went into the kitchen. It was over; his mother was gone. It would have been nice, he thought foolishly, if she had phoned to say goodbye. Now it was only the old man between himself and death. He shivered and drew his robe tighter around him, conscious of a slight belly bulge; he would have to get back to squash at least once a week. He walked to the window and saw, reflected back from the pane, the fleshy contours of his face, the hairline faintly receding, a bit of grey at the temples, signs of a man at the threshold of middle age. He was not sure he liked the circles under his eyes. His sigh was in sorrow not only for his mother but for himself. Then, without warning, it hit him, a nausea to the heart, followed by tears, abrupt, painful, brief.

He put up the coffee, showered and dressed. He checked his office calendar; no problem on Bennett taking over his cases for several days. It was best to go down at once and try to help. Fran would need all the help she could get. He found a number on the address wheel, and dialed long distance.

A dry sardonic voice greeted him. "Good morning. I hope your news is good, considering the hour. Speak up."

"Uncle Victor, it's your favorite aging nephew, with apologies."

"I know. I just got the same call from Fran. It seems my dear talkative sister is gone. Well, she was an old lady and ready to go, or so she said."

"I'll be down later this morning."

"Good. Call me back when you book your flight, I'll meet you at the airport personally. And no long faces, please. Funerals go on here all the time."

12

2.

Fran was back in her room, seated at the edge of the couch, numb, staring ahead into the wall mirror. Her throat was parched, her breathing rapid, eyes glazed in the aftermath of shock. A trembling that she could not control had begun in her arms and legs. *It had to be, we were waiting for it to happen, it had to happen.* She moaned and seemed too bewildered to cry; yet somewhere inside her a scream was forming, a bubble about to burst.

That face seen through the window . . . mother lying there on the bed, eyes shut, hands at her side, skin drawn tight, a death mask . . . lamp upon the night table still lit, its pale illumination reflecting upon the face, that face forcing itself into her mind, the face immobile, unbreathing, nightmarish . . . *It had come, it was here at last, yes they were expecting it . . .*

A great exhaustion overcame her, and she fell back heavily upon the couch. The sudden hush, dappled sunlight on the curtains, light and dark on her eyelids mesmerizing, drawing her mercifully down into sleep.

She was alone, lost in the endless meadow behind the

farm. The barns and the pumphouse were silently watching her. She thought she heard her mother call "Fran . . . cie!" but the summer wind blew the voice in another direction. A soft sky overhead, a hum of insects at her feet. Far away a neighboring farmhouse seemed like a toy against the rim of hills. Now she turned, her eyes sweeping the apple blossoms, not moving, not yet certain which way to go. The waterfall lay in an easterly direction where the stand of maples rose to the distant horizon. That was the landmark, she recalled, those maples that led to the secret place.

She began to move across the meadow. She was ten; school was out early, and she had decided to revisit the waterfall nestled at the end of the forest. It wasn't very large, a dammed-up area, the water spilling over a tier of logs into a shallow rock basin. How mysterious the place seemed to her, the sky close and unreal. Possibly, if the water was warm today, she would take off her clothes and wade in the pool below the falls.

Her father had warned her about straying too far from the house. His fear urged her on. Now she was moving through the rough grass that fringed the meadow. Buttercup and clover brushed her bare ankles; their faint odor swam upward into her head, sickening yet strangely desired. The grass became higher and mixed with burrs and sharp brush, whipping around her waist as she entered into the forest. A low stone fence was her guide; she remembered it and followed its winding course for several hundred yards when it abruptly ended. She stopped. Her eyes peered into the deeper wood; a green-gold haze stretched ahead where the sunlight washed down through the leaves. A birdcall startled her, then a strange silence fell everywhere. She began to run. She remembered the stone wall, but was uncertain from that point where it ended. Nevertheless she plunged on, her feet finding a narrow cowpath. She felt her heart beating.

14

Now she listened as she ran, her ear alert for the sound of the falls. She stopped, again, hoping to surprise the sound by her presence; silence greeted her, broken by a birdcall. For the first time, a tremor of fear touched her limbs. She called out, "Hello!" Why did she do that? It would only draw attention to her . . . from whom? Was there anyone . . . ? She spun around in panic. A faint rustle in the grass. She was aware of the darkening of the forest; the sun was behind a cloud bank, and a wind began to hum through the higher leaves.

She changed course abruptly and ran in the direction that she assumed would lead to a clearing. After several minutes she paused for breath only to realize that she was even in deeper wood than before. She was lost. Tears rushed to her eyes. She called out, "Momma? Where are you? Please find me!" Now she was screaming, "Momma, Momma!"

Fran opened her eyes. A dull pain, lips stinging from her own teeth biting them. She rose and stumbled into the bathroom for some water. The cold liquid on her neck and forehead soothed her. She stared out of the window at the hotel sign blinking in pale daylight neon: ROOMS WEEK OR SEASON. Below, terryrobed bathers, mostly elderly, headed for the beach and the therapeutic waters. She watched them for a moment . . . a flash of the face seen through the window, skin drawn tight, eyes shut, a death mask . . . and her own terror receding. "I have to go back," she whispered, "I must say goodbye to her."

3.

On the plane, Donald thought of his parents reaching their eighties together, finally separated by death. The weight of their existence seemed to reach back to him, the only son, the ridiculous heir to . . . what? A closetful of worn clothes? A packet of faded personal papers?

It was better this way, though for awhile it would be tough on the old man. He was aware on his last yearly visit that their situation had become more alarming. They were a brave but tottering household. Mother holding onto the door so she wouldn't fall; Father forgetting about his son's arrival ten minutes after he entered the room; Mother forgetting to turn off the gas; Father losing his keys; Mother losing her hearing aid; Father hiding his money and upsetting the house in the search; Mother falling; Father getting lost. A comedy of small horrors.

And with each succeeding year, the flights from despair to euphoria had become more pronounced. "I'm dying," Mother would say. "Can't you see it in my face?" And she'd break out into a sly smile. On the phone she'd begin right off with, "This will be the last time you'll hear my voice," while her cheeriness would flash over the line, belying the message. And father would chant behind her, "Where's the money? She stole it but says it's lost. Such a thief for a wife!"

On his last visit, she had confided, "It's coming soon."

"What's coming, Mother?" They were sitting in the small patio behind the apartment house.

"The last sleep. You have no idea how I look forward to it."

Father said, "She'll live to be a hundred. I only want to reach ninety."

"If that man reaches ninety," she replied, "I'll drop dead of shock. Right on the spot!"

It was barely a month ago that her voice hummed over the phone, following a long chime of coins being dropped into the box a thousand miles away—she resolutely refused to call collect—and he asking, "What is it, mother?" And her brisk reply, "Nothing, dear. I just thought you might like to hear my voice. It's so long since you came down. You are a bad boy. Are you busy right now?" Donald said, "Yes, I am, Mother. I'll call you back this evening at eight, at the hall phone. Take care of yourself." He hung up. Had he called her back? Probably not. And she probably might have forgotten as well. She refused to let him install a private phone. "I don't want to sit there every day expecting it to ring." That was her reply whenever he brought the matter up. Maybe she didn't really care to hear from him, literally not be bothered by her children—could that have been the reason? The old lady would have *us* do the worrying, Donald thought; she was mischievous enough. Farewell, Mother, life-giving and eternal no longer . . . .

He leaned back in his seat and sipped the drink. Dick Bennett would cover for him at the office. Debbie, driving him to the airport, insisted on putting a box of hard candy into his briefcase for Father. Donald knew she would have accompanied him on the trip if things had not been so difficult between her and Fran. But that was another matter, never resolved. His mind drifted toward Fran. Mother's burden had been a irritant between them; now, released, could she make peace with him? It had always seemed difficult in the past, a mystery he could not fathom. The truth was, even now, decades after they each had moved away from home into marriages and careers, he could not make a relaxed connection with her. He felt the ache of unfulfilled family matters, long overdue reckonings, that brought on a wave of guilt. Her presence was upon him the instant the wheels touched the runway.

Uncle Victor was waiting at the airport. Still vigorous in his late seventies, he reached for the suitcase as Donald came down the long Arrivals corridor.

"You need a haircut," he began with a brusque charm.

"Look upon me as an unreformed hippie, in spirit at least."

"As long as you still wear shoes. I can't stand grownup men wearing sneakers. You look pretty good. Are you dyeing your hair? Only her doctor knows!" He winked. Donald liked his easy banter and unsentimental view of the world. Once inside the car and under way, Victor became serious. "Are you holding up OK? Good. It's a shock, it wears off. But sister Frances has me worried. The kid sounded strange over the phone. I invited her for breakfast, all I got was a quick message and out."

"Where is she now?" Donald asked, scanning the roadway.

"I don't know. She moves around a lot, last place was the *Ocean Spray*."

"I mean Mother."

Victor laughed quietly. "At the apartment, where else? She couldn't walk away now, but if anyone could, she'd do it." After a moment, he said, "Fran's probably with Poppa."

Donald shook his head in a kind of amused despair. "I guess he's right there minding the body."

"He might even be talking to her. He's used to her not hearing him." Victor chuckled, cleared his throat. "He's alright, the old man, he'll get along. Everybody gets used to this."

"Not that quickly, I'm sure."

They drove in silence, moving across the causeway toward the beach area. The sunlight reflected everywhere, over the water, the whitewashed houses, the heavy-branched trees. To one side of the beach, a facade of large hotels reared up, even from this distance sunbleached and unreal. Something faintly Far Eastern; one was surprised not to see minarets pointing toward the blue cloudless sky. The most deceptive prop of the landscape, the palm tree, lent still another touch of the exotic. When the causeway ended at the south corner of the beach, and the car drove through the rows of small houses and motels, he sensed at last the reality of these streets.

Here lived the elderly who were preparing to die. The disease, simply, was life. The cure was death, tempered by climate. The climate was essential; sunshine and warm air seemed to ease all threats. And so they drifted, even as the days, toward the end. The broken siren of the ambulance rose and fell, close by, or in the distance, answering the call: heart attack, fainting spell, home accident, all the ailments and infirmities of old age.

Knowing this from previous visits, Donald was never-theless surprised at the jaunty step of the pedestrian, the

19

gentle smile upon so many faces; peace, resignation, rarely bitterness. They were the deserted, castoffs of the children, and their ironic expression could be, he thought, a form of revenge by those who know the future too well. They knew that age and the terrors of illness awaited all; the parent's humiliation would in turn be visited upon the children.

An old man, bald and in shorts, was doing pushups in the center of a small tree-lined park along the avenue. Victor slowed the car as they passed. "I once saw him do thirty pushups," he announced, Around the figure, in a circle, some dozen or so elderly women observed and made clucking sounds, some applauding and offering encouraging remarks. The man continued his pushups.

"How old is he?" Donald asked.

"Sixty-five, seventy. He's showing off for the ladies, he wants to be a hero to the very end."

"I suppose a dead hero is still a hero."

"I wouldn't be surprised one day to see an old grandmother slide right under him just for a laugh. They love to play sexy games. A lot of these oldies can still get it up. I've heard complaints by the grandmothers that they're often molested by strange grandfathers." He grinned, peering over the wheel, eyes darting quickly from left to right. "I hate to drive. I get dizzy spells. I'm no youngster myself. How long do you think I've got left?"

Donald ventured a humorous guess. "Another fifty."

"Any week, any day, when you're past seventy-five." He cleared his throat. "And I'll tell you, sonny, when you lose your feeling for women, you're through no matter what age." Donald wasn't listening, but Victor rattled on. "I guess I'm half-through. You know the old joke, 'Just put me on top, I can get off by myself.' "

Same old Victor, same old gags, they'd probably get

worse as the days wore on, Donald thought, pained at this insensitivity.

"Let me tell you," he continued. "When I'm ready to go, I'll go. I make the decision. I have a little pill, sonny. They won't keep me alive just to suffer. When the time comes, one swallow and that's it."

"How'd you manage that, Uncle? I thought only spies and astronauts get those quick-exit pills."

"Well, I got one." He winked. "Right in the little box with my gold cuff links." He turned into a street of smaller apartment complexes, slowing his speed. "I didn't stop by earlier, decided to wait for you. The old man and I never got along too well. I stay away as much as possible."

Donald asked, "What about funeral arrangements? I think they have burial plots somewhere."

"It's all changed. Cremation. No fuss, no robbery. Why spend a thousand dollars for a casket with fake silver trim? Who'll come visit the grave? Not very often, if you do."

"I guess not. If you arranged it, that's fine."

"It's all a racket, this funeral business, believe me."

"What about the ashes?" He hesitated. "I mean . . ."

Victor gave him a quick glance. "You want the ashes?"

"Yes." Donald swallowed dryly. "I'd like that." A cupful of her spirit, a pinch of her flesh, in her dust an echo of the voice he knew so well.

"There's the house just ahead." Victor whistled a tune without embarrassment. "She's better off, remember that. She was in and out of hospitals all year."

He carefully pulled to the curb. *Venetian Gardens*. On the sign a painted gondola to ease the lodgers into the final sunset. Next to it: *Eden Apartments*. A local artist's version of Paradise, muscle-flexing Adam and nude Eve, apple in hand, under a palm tree.

"How do you feel?" asked Victor.

"A little queasy."

"Don't let the body upset you. Or Fran if she's there."

They entered the *Eden* hallway, past an arrangement of yellowed potted palms, past a dozen doors of two-room apartments that led off the dim corridor. Through the doors and transoms came the odors of cooking, or the odors were already in the hall, impregnated in the wood, so that no amount of scrubbing could erase them completely. Donald had on each visit been struck anew by this mingling of odors, and now the smell seemed to make his mission more trying and absurd. In the presence of death, he wished all cooking to cease, all movement to slow down, all speech to be muted.

At the end of the empty silent corridor, with Victor close behind, he stopped at Number 5. He was strangely fearful. He listened at the door and heard nothing. Where was the old man? Asleep in his favorite chair? Perhaps. Possibly waiting for her to wake from her afternoon nap. With a nod at Victor, he knocked softly. No answer. He tried again, a slight push, the door opened. The narrow kitchen was empty. They entered and peered into the adjoining bedroom, empty as well. On the bed and couch lay scattered magazines, articles of clothing, an enema bag, a pair of slippers, magnifying glass, miniature electric batteries.

Donald called out, "Is anyone home?"

Victor said, "I guess they took away the body."

A splashing sound from the bathroom, its door ajar. They turned in one motion. Donald took several hestitant steps toward the door. A wild thought raced through his head.

A voice—drifting in from the window? the transom?—that sounded shockingly familiar carried across the air. "Are you back, you awful man, filling the tub and helping me in but where were you all this time? Or is it you, Fran?"

Donald pushed the door open wider. There, seated in the tub, a small bony figure, her back toward him, was Mother. She was cheerfully talking to herself as she cupped the water with her hands and poured it down her back and arms. "You awful man, is there anything left of your mind? It's sad even when a monster gets old because you're a monster to leave me this way."

"Mother, is that you?" he asked numbly, leaning against the door.

She turned, her mouth opened, minus her lower plate, as she reached to the floor for a towel. A dim but unmistakable light now leaped to her eyes. "Donnie? Is it Donnie? When did you come? Fran didn't say a word. Dear, what a surprise!"

Stunned, his mind racing with possible explanations (was this one of Fran's games?), Donald stepped into the small bathroom. He leaned down, suffocated by her closeness, and kissed her on the back of her neck. "It's good to see you, mother."

"Oh Donnie, I'm so glad you're here." She reached over to grasp his arm, and whispered, "I'm so glad you came. Your father's been trying to kill me."

4.

Donald walked the neighboring streets looking for his father, but Fran stayed on his mind. The phone call and its false message worried him. It was, he suspected, an emotional outburst that had to do with getting him to come here, a hysteria of some sort which he could not explain. She needed continual support, he knew that, and she found ways to remind him every so often that he was part of the family. Well, he was here, and that reminder was even a bit welcome.

He spotted the old man seated on a bench beneath twin palm trees, a favorite spot. Six months, perhaps more, had gone by since their last meeting; he felt the shock of age. His father appeared smaller as Donald approached, an odd grimace stamped on his face by years of exposure to sunlight.

"Hello, Dad."

The figure on the bench looked up, startled, the mouth opening to reveal his last two yellow teeth, then relaxed into a shy smile. "Is that you, son? How are you?" His one good eye blinked.

"Fine. And you?"

"Pretty good, I'm holding up. When did you get here?"

"An hour or so ago. I thought it was time for a visit."

"She'd like that, your mother," he said. "Did you stop in at the house?"

"Yes. And you weren't there."

"How could I be there if I'm here?" He smiled roguishly.

"You left Momma in the bathtub."

"I left her there?" Surprise, not alarm.

"I expected to find Fran at the house."

He scratched his chin. "Is she still in the tub. Did she drown?"

Donald had to laugh. "No, I helped her out, but if she doesn't get a bad cold I'll be surprised."

"She never gets a cold," he replied with vigor, propelled to his feet. "She's very strong, don't let her fool you. The last time she was in the hospital, the doctors said she had the body of a fifty-year-old woman. And she's eighty. Maybe eighty-five. Her heart and lungs, the doctors said, were perfect."

"That may be so. But you can't leave her in a tub of water and go out for hours."

"I was out for ten minutes."

"One hour. It's a good thing I came by. Come on, she's waiting for you."

"She can float, did you know that?" He chirped in a high voice. "I found her floating once, you wouldn't believe it, after I got home from shopping. I think she was asleep in the water." He laughed and did a little shuffle with his feet, then reached out to hold onto Donald's arm. "Oh, she won't drown, not that girl!"

They started walking slowly. "How are you these days, Pa? You look pretty good."

"Good and then sometimes not good. I'm better than she

is. She's on her way out. She won't reach ninety, you can be sure. Just as well, just as well. Are you having a nice visit? When did you arrive?"

"Just now."

"Today? Wasn't it yesterday?"

"You see, Pa, this thing about your memory . . . You're walking around, not knowing the hour or day, it isn't safe. You leave Momma alone for hours—"

"She likes to be alone. She told me that." He was emphatic.

"OK. But you can't leave her in the tub. Is that clear? And last month her dress caught fire, how did that happen?"

"Her dress? She leaned over the gas stove and the belt began to burn. Lucky I saw it. How did you know?"

"Fran wrote to me. I guess Momma told her. But what it means, you have to watch her, take care of her—"

He nodded vigorously. "You're right. She's old. She's very old. The other day we were talking about it, who's older than who, and anyway how can you prove it? We lost the birth certificates long ago."

They passed the Island National Bank where father had his safe deposit box, subject of much speculation in the family.

"The same thing with your safe deposit box," Donald said. "You were going to take care of it, but you didn't."

The old man thought: The bank! I knew he'd get to that. They sent him there. Well, I won't sign those papers.

Donald took his arm and led him to another bench. They sat down. "Let's rest a few minutes, would you like that? Now, Poppa, we went to the bank last year because of this whole problem of your safe deposit box and what to do about it, remember? You have things, private things in the box, insurance or bank books, it doesn't matter what. But

26

what if something happens to you? Nobody can get into that box now except you."

"That's right," he replied. "No one."

"But if something happens—"

"What will happen?"

"If you go to the hospital, or get hurt, for example. Or suppose one day you just forget where your bank is. That would be funny. You have the box and no one knows where it is. Because you changed your bank many times, you told me."

He nodded. "But I left all instructions—"

"Yes, but if you change your bank say next month, after I go back, and then something happens, where will we find the book, or the key?"

"You'll look for it. You'll find it somewhere."

Was he kidding? No, the old boy didn't want to make it easy for them. He was playing out his last game. Who the hell knows what he has in his box anyway? It could be cash, a ten-dollar bank balance, some cuff links, maybe a pipe, photographs of the farm, God knows what . . .

Donald continued, "We thought, Fran and I, that one of the children should have a key, or the power of attorney, in order to protect you. Now you agreed to it last time. You were going to have the bank send me the papers."

"They didn't?"

"No. You didn't tell them." Exasperation crept into his voice. "You have to authorize them legally, sign a paper, understand, Poppa? It's for your own protection."

A moment of silence. "If I give you a duplicate key, she'll get it."

"Who?"

"Your mother. She'll get hold of it and poke around."

"Don't you trust me, for Christsakes?"

"It's her I don't trust. She's scheming all the time. She

schemed to steal my money for her father and brothers. I won't forget that." He turned softer, apologetic. "It's her, don't you see, not you." He gripped his knees, and said thoughtfully, "Anyway, you'll come down here if I die, won't you? You'll take care of everything."

Donald shook his head, was about to speak, but instead rose. The old man wasn't going to knock him off his balance, not this early in his visit. "Let's go. Mother will worry what happened to both of us."

Crossing the street, they were confronted by an elderly whitehaired man arguing with a policeman about to hand him a ticket, to the amusement of a small group of mostly elderly bystanders.

"You can read the sign," said the policeman. "It says 'No Jaywalking'."

"I can read, sure," exclaimed the man. "But I left my glasses home. What should I do if I forget my glasses?"

"Here's the ticket. Now take it like a good citizen. We can't have old fellas like yourself crossing against the lights and getting hurt, heh?"

"Are you telling me where to cross? Before you were born I was crossing the streets." He stammered angrily. "I'm seventy-eight years old and nobody should tell me where to cross!" He tore up the ticket with a flourish. Ragged applause, a murmur of apprehension from the listeners. Father, halting at the edge of the crowd, called out, "We'll cross whenever we want. We'll stop traffic. We'll all get heart attacks and fill your hospitals!"

More applause. Donald pulled him away, smiling weakly at the policeman. "Come on," he whispered.

"We're not afraid of their tickets," father said gleefully. "They can't tell us what to do."

At the door of the apartment, Donald said, "You stay with mother. I'll be back soon. I want to check Fran."

"You'll be back?"

"Yes."

"Because we like to see you, son. We don't have much to talk about, but we're glad when you come to visit us." He nodded shyly.

"Now Pa, was Fran here at all this morning?"

"Yes, she came by a little later than usual. Then she went off again, no idea where and just as well."

"See you soon." Reaching the street, he thought, What the hell am I going to say to her?

5.

The *Ocean Spray* was one of the dozens of small hotels scattered within the area. The entrance, in faded blue pastel, the paint chipped, did not appear inviting. On the small open porch a number of residents rocked or dozed in ancient rattan furniture. Inside, a sour musty smell radiated from the walls, the floors, the ceiling; it told of decades of painted surfaces, one over the other, each drying with the earlier smells imbedded like a dye. The usual massive TV set hung above the door, flickering with images and sound; colors flared out from the picture tube, flowing over into one another, a companion blight to the painted walls.

The desk clerk raised his head from the pages of a newspaper as he languidly mulled over Donald's query. "Yes," he answered, "The name's familiar. She checked out about a month ago. Just a minute, let's see my books." He reached into a drawer for a faded ledger, opened it and moved his finger down a row of names. "Here it is, yep, a month ago."

"Did she leave a forwarding address?"

He shook his head. "Certain type of people don't. I mean, they move around with the season, y'know? She was a nice lady." He suddenly laughed. "She hated the TV, said it was ruining people, ruining their minds, which may be right except most people have no minds to begin with, don't you think? Like me, for instance. If I had a mind, would I be working here?"

"Well, thanks anyway," Donald said, turning to leave.

The clerk called after him, "Why not try the *Mercury* couple of blocks west. Lots of itinerants use it. *Mercury*—they should call it Lead!"

He left the lobby and its stale air. The word "itinerant" stung him. Yes, he had to admit it fit his sister, drifting from hotel to hotel, finding a life in ephemeral activities: art courses, lectures, looking up friends in nearby or distant cities—a fruitless return to old places, old scenes, a vague search for "meaning." She was once a believer in political causes, but that fanaticism weakened; in its place grew a haunting sorrow of the past. In earlier years, her walls had been covered with magazine photos of the atrocities of the world: starving children in India, the bombed victims of Hiroshima, and then the Vietnam horror, the napalmed child on fire fleeing down the road. The cruelty of history pressed upon her; perhaps that explained her moving from place to place, as though looking for an unscarred land-scape, a psychic refuge within a natural one.

She would decide to work toward a college degree, then quit after a semester. She moved in and out of therapy, lost in a smattering of quick phrases that she liked to throw at him when they'd meet. After her divorce, her visits to their parents kept getting longer, until she simply decided to stay on. For awhile this change lifted her spirits. She enjoyed the warm climate and soon was riding around on a bike each day or strolling to the beach. But before long she became

31

moody, preoccupied, uncertain. Often, when he flew down, irritation about herself and the family leaped into open arguments, resulting in name-calling and tears.

Why did she choose to live this way, he thought sadly, and make everyone feel they were somehow responsible for her. She would leave, then return, like a child running back home after each disaster. And yet, Donald sensed this refuge was a trap; she wanted others inside the trap, especially him. "Let's talk about mother," she would say, "*our* mother," meaning, I have done my part all these years and where were you?

He checked the *Mercury*; they suggested trying the *Sea Breeze* farther down the street, a popular place for singles and divorcees. At the *Sea Breeze* a desk clerk flipped some cards, then said, "She's in 308."

He tried the house phone but there was no answer. The clerk said, "She didn't go out since I came on. Maybe she's not taking calls, y'know?"

"I'm her brother. If it's OK with you, I'll try the doorbell."

"If that won't wake her, nothing will. Go ahead."

Donald took the elevator to the third floor, walked to door 308 and knocked. There was no reply. He pushed the buzzer, then knocked again. "Fran, it's me. Donald." His voice was urgent. "Everything's OK. Open the door."

The lock turned, the door swung back, and she was standing before him. He took in her tired face, still with its attractive contours, the nose and chin well-proportioned, the mouth expressive, and the eyes—those blue questioning eyes which held the shadows of unfading memory. Her blonde hair fell uncombed to her shoulders. A youthful beauty still lingered; it was a face not yet ready to accept age, despite the faint lines around eyes and mouth, a full-ness before the turn that held its own appeal and drew its

32

share of glances from men. How thin she looked. Seeing her again, the thought of her difficulties struck him sharply, his irritations vanished: he was aware only of her loneliness, and of his past affection for her. They embraced.

"Oh, Donnie, I'm so glad you're here!" She kissed him and clung to him for a moment. He felt a tremor of his old dependence, a reminder of her dominance and once-held authority of childhood.

"Just relax. Everything's fine." He led her inside and closed the door.

"You saw Momma?"

"Yes."

"I know you'll think I'm crazy after what happened . . ."

"Well, Fran, after all . . . You said she was dead!"

"I couldn't help it, I thought she was dead. When I went by this morning and looked in at the window," her voice rising, "I could have sworn that—"

"It's all right, OK, things like that happen."

"Her face was a mask, the skin, the lips, it looked like a death mask."

"Still, shouldn't you have gone inside and checked before you made the call, hell, six-thirty in the morning—"

"I guess I panicked. I just ran." A tight laugh broke from her. "Was Momma playing some kind of trick on me, I wonder? How else can you explain it?" She rose and moved tensely across the room, her face drained of color. "And in the confusion I didn't call you back. I'm sorry."

"Look, we all make mistakes. A deep sleep often looks like death. Hallucination. Everybody gets them, even lawyers." He reached over and placed a hand on her shoulder in a gesture of understanding. She gripped it.

"I'm glad you're here, Donnie. I'm so alone most of the time."

Donald sat down and lit a cigarette. "Why don't we

forget all that and just say I came down for a family visit. Which I should have done earlier. I'm here. Period. Now what else is new?"

"God, you don't expect to find anything new here, do you?"

"Right. Let's stay with the old. Climate the same. Parents the same, just getting older, bumbling around in a couple of tiny rooms, falling over one another. The stove is dangerous, not to mention a few other things."

"And you're blaming me."

"I'm not. Why should I?" he replied.

"I'm doing all I can, whatever one can do."

"I'm sure you are. And I know it isn't easy."

"How would you know? You're never here," she said with a bite of sarcasm. "Except when it's convenient for you."

Donald shook his head in mild despair. "Come on now, Fran, let's not get into that subject."

"You have never, never, thought of anyone but yourself!"

"I have thought of our parents as much as you have."

"From where? A thousand miles away? With your fancy clients, your friends who drink all the time and exchange wives. I know what goes on in your business!"

He gripped the edge of his chair. "You phoned and I caught the first plane out. I'm a thousand miles away because I happen to live a thousand miles away. You live here. Maybe you enjoy being a martyr, how the hell do I know? Maybe you want this burden to the very end. For God's sake, you've been their maid for how many years—six, seven, eight?"

"Who else will do it?" She was sullen now.

"Qualified people. You can still see them, visit them, it may not be the perfect solution but it's not the snake pit either."

34

"They're together now. Don't you see that?" She spoke firmly. "As long as they're together they can make it, each one supports the other. In a Home, you never know what happens psychologically. They can go to pieces."

"You tell me if they aren't going to pieces this way."

"It's different. They have the illusion of some kind of family life. If we break that illusion, don't you see . . .? If you were here, day by day, you'd know what I mean." She sighed, her voice trailing off. "With all the jokes about this city, it isn't the worst. The climate is lovely. I just thought the other day"—she shot him an appealing look—"that you're so close here to your office up north, and with all those flights, you could think of operating partly from here."

"It wouldn't work," he said flatly. "There's just no point to it."

"The point is our parents. Your living here part of the time would be a big boost to them, not to mention helping me in this situation. Having you nearby would be such a comfort, Donnie."

"I don't think it's a sound idea," he said. "For one thing, Debbie wouldn't go along." He was uncomfortable with this preposterous idea. "She's sympathetic to the problem here, but I know her feeling about making any kind of move."

"We all know her feeling about me."

"It's not you."

"It is me," Fran insisted.

"Then you might try and figure out why," he retorted bluntly. "Debbie always tried to be your friend, but you managed to make things difficult."

"Exactly how did I do that?" She regarded him belligerently. "Exactly how, if you don't mind."

"You'll have to figure it out by yourself. Let's drop it."

35

"Debbie began to distrust me when she found out a sister could be more concerned than a wife. Well, I'm not ashamed of that."

"You tried to break up my marriage, for Christsake!"

"How did I—"

"A lot of ways, and some not so subtle. We're not going into it. Period!"

Her chin trembled. "Oh, Donnie, why are we quarreling? We were once so close." Tears came to her eyes. "We used to sit and talk for hours about literature and art and life. Even when I was married, way back to number one, Rocky, he used to say, 'Why don't your kid brother move in with us, he's around so much of the time.' Remember those times? And now, I'm alone with so many thoughts and feelings I can't express. Those times when I'd write you, I hoped you'd answer my questions, but maybe you didn't understand them. I didn't know myself, I still don't know clearly what it is, except something is there, inside me, that wants to be heard. As though I want someone to say it for me. Maybe you, Donnie. I could never speak to her, our own mother. Or Poppa. I'm scared at what I might say to them if it burst out. Momma marrying me off when I was sixteen, that was murder, do you know that?" She was breathing heavily, her words rushing forward. "I was too young, the whole thing was crazy. Just to get me off her back and out of the house. And now, a lifetime later, I'm in the house again . . ."

Donald listened, trying to sort out the welter of emotion pouring from her. What did she mean by "something that wants to be heard?" A strange turbulence gripped her during his recent visits. He could only listen and look on helplessly. Too much time to be bridged, too much distance between them. He watched as she walked to the window, drawing her robe closer about her, lips together as if to suppress an unspoken history whose terror was known only to herself.

"Fran," he said, then hesitated. He had to be careful of his words, he could not bear to use the wrong words to further upset her and cause her pain. "That's all behind you, dear. Can't you see it that way?"

"Nothing is ever behind you." Her voice was calm, as though it were another day and a new conversation, and she in control. "It keeps coming up in front of you again, just when you think it's gone. No, you wouldn't know that. Your life has been too easy."

"Please listen to me, dear—"

"Am I dear to you? That was long ago perhaps, when we were younger. Now it's all hypocrisy." The room was quiet, except for the low hum of an air conditioner. Outside the window, a group of trees swayed in the light wind. She nodded toward them. "Aren't those trees beautiful? They're more beautiful than people. I sometimes wish I could talk to them, I bet they'd listen. People don't really listen."

"Except brothers. They have no choice."

She offered a tentative smile. "Yes. But now that you paid your visit, you'll probably turn right around and go back."

"I might just decide to stick around till the weekend. Humor the old folks."

"And me. You could take me to dinner, for example. I bet you have a dozen credit cards." He could see the whole idea delighted her, that his arrival was an event around which she could construct her own little family.

"You mean a smart girl like you can't get a credit card date in this town?"

"Are you kidding?" she replied. "I have very few men friends, no one special."

"Then go out and hunt one or two."

"I thought of it, maybe I'm scared, or out of practice." She cast a swift glance at the mirror. "You won't believe it, I got a letter from Betty who heard on the family grapevine that my ex-hubby is down here. Rocky the One."

"Rocky? You mean he lives here, or is it a week's excursion to the races?

"He moved down last year. Seems his wife has some kind of illness." She spread her arms in a nervous gesture. "So there you are."

Donald sensed a subtle excitement in her, despite her seemingly casual manner of introducing the subject. "Why don't you look him up? He was a nice guy, always good for some laughs. You said you had no friends here."

"You mean ex-husbands can be friends?" She feigned surprise. "I have to admit he wasn't a bad husband, just a general washout. If we hadn't been such kids it might even have worked out. It's water over the dam now." She paused, as if the whole subject was a mistake and not to be taken seriously.

Donald moved to the door. "I might look him up just for old times sake. You wouldn't mind?"

"Why should I?" The slightest hesitation. "He's in the phone book. I checked."

"I might do that, if the mood strikes."

"Just don't mention my name."

He winked. "Attorneys never divulge their sources." He kissed her lightly. "We have a dinner date. I'll run along and let you rest, while I play the tourist and maybe take a swim. We both had a rough day so far."

"It's still strange, me and Momma this morning . . . as if I dreamed it." She shuddered. "I feel I'm just coming awake."

"Pick you up at seven. Forget Momma."

"Hey, I'll wear my new hat." Her eyes were shining.

"Tell you what, before we get into any more discussions about the folks, which will get us nowhere, let's take them on a picnic. Tomorrow or the next day. How about it?"

"I don't think they'll agree."

"We'll kidnap them. You tie up the old lady and I'll knock out Poppa."

She laughed, her first real laugh of the day. "Donnie, how can you talk that way? They're our parents after all!"

6.

They were preparing to take their daily nap when Father spoke. "I wonder why he's here? What does he want?"

"Who?"

"Our son. Donald."

A silence. Then Mother said, "Francie hasn't been here for two days."

"Was Donald the second, or the eldest?"

"Fran is the eldest, don't you remember?"

"He looks odd. He doesn't look a bit like me. Of course, you tell me I'm the father . . . " He sat up. "Are you listening to me?"

"Yes. I can hear you very well when it's quiet."

"Where's the machine?"

"I'm wearing it. It's not turned on, though. I'm saving the battery. Now, are you going to give Donald your money to take care of ?"

"Ha, ha. You too. What money? What are you talking about?"

"Whatever you have in your bank box."

"Whatever I have is my own business, not yours, or his."
He noisily swallowed some water from the glass on his
night-table. "Dollinger, that was his name! Louis
Dollinger."

"Yes, I remember him. What a dear man he was," she
murmured.

"He could have been the boy's father."

"Go to sleep."

"I was away on a trip, and he was there when I got back."

"He came by to borrow some sugar."

"Sugar! You gave away sugar, salt, bread, vinegar, on-
ions. And he gave you his carrot maybe? His big red
carrot?"

"I don't hear a word you're saying."

"So he's the boy's father. Or Fran's. One of them for sure.
From the very beginning you flirted with other men. And
all the time as if nothing was in your head, but plenty was in
your head. Carrots! Wasn't my carrot good enough for you?
You wanted to be a whore but didn't have the guts."

"I hear every word you're saying, you vile man."

"And that son of yours is here, God knows why. I don't
trust him."

"Why do you say that? You love him."

A silence spread within the room like a mist, settling
everywhere, muffling the street noises, even the ticking
clock. The old man snorted, spat, then moved his legs over
the edge of the couch. "Do you think I love him?" She
didn't reply. She was already drifting off to sleep, and his
voice barely reached her.

She said softly, "I hope you shut off the burner. Did you
do that? And remember when you go to the store to get me
a new set of batteries."

"Why do you say I love the boy? It never occurred to
me."

"Not the flat batteries, the round ones. Fran knows how to take care of these things. She's very loyal, but forgetful. She isn't very happy. Do you notice that?"

Father rose from the couch and crossed to the kitchen. "It's too late for a nap, and Donald's coming. Get up. I'll make some tea."

"I can still take forty winks."

"Why don't you sit in the rocker? You'll sleep later."

"I might not feel sleepy later." But she slipped out of bed, found her robe, and settled into the rocker.

"How would you like it, dear?"

"With a lump of sugar, please."

"Coming up, coming up. I always wanted to be a singing waiter."

"Well, not here, I hope. But you do serve tea nicely."

"Never dropped a cup yet. Maybe the kettle, but not the cup."

The water had hardly begun to boil when Donald arrived, and soon they were all seated sipping tea.

"How nice to be together," said Mother. "I hope Fran will show up."

"Don't hope, it will come true," chimed in Father.

"Remember to thank your sweet wife for those candies."

"They were sent for me, and you've eaten half already," said Father.

"They're for both of you, really, Debbie loves you both."

"And your wonderful son?" Mother asked. "How is he?"

"Fine, when we hear from him. That's only when he needs money." Donald laughed. He was relaxed after a good night's sleep, and enjoying the sun. "How do you like my one-day tan?"

"That's impossible," Father exclaimed. "Nobody can get a tan in one day."

"Is that all he's been here, a day?"

"Two days, Mother. This is my second day."

"Two days. Did you hear that?" And she turned to Father.

"Of course I hear. It's you who has trouble hearing."

"Not when my batteries are strong. Right now, my batteries are weak, but I hear very well."

"I left five sets of batteries last time, Mother," said Donald with some annoyance. "What happened to them?"

She thought for a moment. "I gave two to the lady upstairs, they fitted her machine exactly. Then I left one on too long. I think I lost another one. That leaves this one in the machine. Sometimes it works and sometimes it doesn't."

Father guffawed. "It's not the hearing aid. It's your ears. Sometimes they work, and then not. Throw the damn machine away. What's the difference whether you hear or not? You're not going anywhere."

She sighed. "Still it's nice to know you can hear when you want to. Did I tell you, Donnie, when I had my last examination in the hospital, the doctor told me my vital organs were like a fifty year old. Imagine!"

"That's very good, Mother."

"Yes, well, what's the point? " Father cut in. "She still wets the bed."

She sat up sharply. "I do not wet the bed."

"Yes you do. And the landlord is complaining about the smell."

"Shit on the landlord, dear."

"Maybe he thinks you're going to do that next." They both laughed.

"Where's the rubber sheet Fran got for you?" asked Donald. "I thought it solved the problem."

43

"It was too hot. I threw it away."

"That was wrong," said Father. "You can't just pee in bed like you're a baby."

She regarded him mischievously. "If I pee in the bath, why not the bed? But I pee in the bath only when you're late in getting me out."

As they talked and argued, taunting one another in a kind of love play, Donald felt a confusion, an inability to fathom the events which constituted their lives. What was going to happen to them? Mother's health had deteriorated generally the past year, while Father had been found more than once wandering around the area unable to remember his address. Yet they could not understand his concern for their future. Or was it that their minds had removed the future, and held only the present?

"Now, both of you, please listen," he said, pushing his cup to one side. "Fran and I are worried about you. We wondered if it might not be best to be in a place where you can get care if it becomes necessary."

"I'm not going anywhere!" Father rose, jarring the table with his fist, for this was a scene he enjoyed. "The last time you were here, we decided no. I'm not old enough for that."

Mother said, "If we wait until we're older, dear, they won't take us."

"If you can crawl to their door, just breathing, they'll take you." He laughed, immediately joined by Mother; they cackled like chickens. "I heard somebody left a dead body at a nursing home, and they took him in. At reduced rates." More and prolonged laughter.

Donald listened unhappily, his confusion mounting; there was nothing he could do but listen, as neither was paying any attention to him.

Mother said wistfully, "I hear they bathe and powder you in a Home, just like in a hospital."

"Go on then," Father pouted. "If you want that, go. Do I look like I'm ready for a Home?"

Mother was fiddling with her hearing aid. "You look like you're ready for the grave."

Father turned to Donald. "You see? She claims she needs new batteries for her hearing aid, but she heard me clearly."

"What did you say, dear?"

"You hear me, you hear every word."

"I hear you now because you're shouting."

"You hear me even when I'm thinking. You're a witch!"

Mother blinked. "What in God's name is he talking about? Right now the batteries are weak, but I hear him. I never know about the batteries."

Father brought over half a grapefruit on a plate, and leaned close to her. "Do you want to eat a grapefruit?"

"For me?"

"It's for you. Do you want it?"

"First say you love me." She pouted and looked ghastly. "I want your son to hear it."

"Daddy love you," he mimicked. "Every day. Every minute."

"Oh, what a liar!" She swiped at him and missed, then accepted the grapefruit and they both sat there sucking the juice from the separate halves. Mother did fairly well with her store teeth; Father had to work a bit more. He boasted of his one remaining tooth in both lower and upper jaw, and used them with uncanny skill although his diet was mainly liquid-soaked food. There they sat, like two patient children, with puckered mouths tugging at the grapefruit pulp. They seemed oblivious to his presence.

"Do you like it?" Father inquired.

"Very delicious."

"Would you like to take your bath?"

"You want to try and drown me again, it that it?" Her eyes closed, she rocked at the edge of the chair, a coy figure.

"Why would I try to drown you? You're not insured, ha, ha." He rose and opened the refrigerator.

"I hope your son is listening," she murmured.

Donald groaned softly, fighting a sense of unreality.

Father rattled some bottles in the refrigerator. "No sir, I'm not going anywhere except in a box." He stopped, peering inside. "Where's that can of beer?"

"You drank it," said Mother.

"I did not drink it," he snapped. "Did you drink it, son?"

"No. I never drink during the day. But I might begin soon."

Father cast a suspicious look. "I just don't like you to steal like your sister. She comes in at night and steals oranges from the refrigerator, did you know that? The stealing has got to stop!"

"Will you be quiet about those oranges? What if she does borrow an orange now and then? Is that a crime?"

"You're used to stealing. Your brother was a thief, except he didn't steal oranges, but money."

"If you keep picking on my family, I'll leave you. I'll get on a bus and ride away, you monster!" She sniffed, as though close to tears.

Donald crossed the room and looked wearily out of the window. A warm flow of air drifted into the room. There was a silence behind him, persisting, enlarging. After a moment he turned, about to speak, then stopped, his mouth closing in a smile. They were both asleep. Suddenly, serenely, Father at the table, Mother in the rocker, their energy had simply run out; they seemed like dolls that needed winding. His heart flowed out toward them in a surge of affection. It was a feeling he could not understand, yet at that moment he was willing to die for them.

Father in the chair, head to one side, his breath shallow and uneven. And Donald's mind alive with memories of childhood . . . .

I would follow him across the fields of farmland, watching his strong hands on the reins of the horses pulling the stoneboat heavy with boulders. And once, riding atop the boulders, they bolted and threw me off, and this man tied one horse to a tree and beat him with the harness until the blood showed through the dark hide. Yes, my father heaving me high into a haywagon, laughing as I sank into the stifling prickly odor of cut meadowgrass, his laughter easing my terror, and everywhere the summer heat now brought back with the room's heat and my own breathing. I had seen that frail arm, limp now at his side, once drive a wedge through a railroad tie, splintering it with a stroke. His strength protected me, I grew with that power inside me. And now, I could smash him with a stroke. But I did not want to destroy him; rather, dimly fathomed, I wanted to give him back what he had given me. How was I to do this? He seemed like a fading luminescent plant, his head a bulb on a bending stalk.

And Mother, dozing at the threshold of death, lying there as innocent as a child, at that moment trusting the world only as a child would, defenseless, unaware of danger. And I, once her child, cradled in those withering arms; then they were firm and warm, and how many times did I run into those arms that smothered me deliciously against her body, her breasts, until I would feel faint at the odor. Those arms, like his, kept all dangers away.

Should I move to her side, bend and kiss her? Oh God if she awoke how would I explain it? She had been a whirlwind in the family, scattering people like objects, then setting them straight again, pretending there had been little if any damage. She had fastened with an insatiable plan upon Frances, her eldest, steering her into a youthful marriage doomed at the first encounter; she moved through events, dragging them behind her. Yet it was never wreckage she saw but a charming disarray of blocks. Are you dreaming, dear Mother, of your crimes? But you know, you know! . . .

He would let them sleep. He thought of shifting the pillow behind his mother's head, but decided against it. Would they leap from their places, laughing gleefully, the moment he closed the door? He could not shake the feeling they were playing out a little scene for him, entertaining him. Outside, in the sunlight, nostalgia gnawed at his gut.

7.

It didn't seem possible, one thousand miles away, some thirty years later, to be seeing Ralph, alias Rocky, his clothes neat and in style, his hair thinning but combed, strolling toward the small seafront park where they had agreed to meet.

Donald waited until that still familiar figure was almost upon him before calling out, "If it isn't Rocky, it's his twin brother. Am I right?"

Rocky stopped, did a mock stare, and broke into astonished laughter. "Knock me over with a feather if it isn't Daring Don!"

"Jesus, I haven't heard that name for a hundred years." They embraced awkwardly. Donald had a fond memory of this blunt, good-hearted man.

"I bet you forgot how you got that nickname, heh? It was on a twenty-foot diving board, you did a backflip and hit the water like a flat duck. Daring Don! Hey, kid, you look great."

"I ought to tell you, Rocky, I never did anything daring after that dive. I'm a coward, always was."

"So, who gives a shit. You're makin' a living, right?" He sat alongside Donald on the bench. "I gotta say that getting your phone call was a surprise. First I thought it was some joker using your name, because how many people come outa the woodwork after what is it, twenty-five, thirty years? So it was crazy cousin Betty, yours not mine, who told you, heh? What a gossip."

Donald laughed. "You must have impressed her to keep track of you all these years. She had a crush on you way back."

"Your family had its share of loonies." He found a toothpick in his shirt pocket and twirled it around his teeth. "Still got that head of hair, I see."

"You don't look so bad yourself."

"Yeah, but aside from the clothes . . . And my hair is goin' if you'll notice." He shook his head. "This is wild, meeting you here. You're not down here escaping the law, are you?"

"That wouldn't be too hard, being a lawyer."

"You down here on a case?"

"Not as simple as that. It's my folks, both pretty old."

Rocky whistled. "They still alive? I thought by this time God woulda called up the old lady to give Him some laughs. She's what, eighty?"

"Pushing it, or over. She won't say."

"And the old boy? Still suspicious of the world?"

"Still hanging on with one or two teeth."

"You're wondering," Rocky said after a pause, "what I'm doing here. I'm retired, sort of. I hurt my back, other problems, saved a little money, some pension, bit of insurance, and here I am. Also, the main reason is my wife. She's kinda arthritic, the climate is right for her." He sighed, replaced his toothpick with a cigarette and carefully lit it. "Smoke?"

"Mostly cigars."

50

He chuckled. "So you'll live a year longer. To me, enjoy what you can enjoy. You play the horses? I bet not."

Donald shook his head. Same old Rocky, clothes, horses, living out his definition of the "good life" and no reason to believe it wasn't as good as any other.

"Still married?"

"Yes."

"Same one?"

"Right."

Rocky was awed. "Guys like you make guys like me look bad. This is number three for me. But I'll never forget Fran, she was number one and not just the number. I was too young to know what the fuck I was doin' and I always felt a little guilty about her. Aah, marriage is for older people. The kids today have the right idea, float around, stay with what you like as long as you like it. You agree?"

"Sure I do, but it can't help any of us older guys now."

He nodded, then softly, "How is Fran?"

"Fran? Well, up and down. She's living here now."

"She's here, in town?" His eyes took on a flash of interest.

"Most of the time, yes. Keeps a watch on the folks."

"How's her health?" Rocky's hand trembled as he flipped the cigarette away.

"She seems OK."

"Does she know I'm here?"

"I don't know."

His face darkened. He shook his head unhappily. "I think about those days sometimes, but there's no point in talking about it. I tried my best. I liked the kid—well, she was just a kid when we got married. I don't think she was ready. I wasn't ready, hell knows. Nobody's ready, to tell the truth. And your old lady pushing us to tie the knot. I guess she figured Fran with her rheumatic heart, if not me who else if they found out, y'see? But she was wrong." He thought for a moment. "Fran could've got anybody, bad heart or good heart. Except she was shy. And being sick she wasn't goin' out grabbin' fellas to marry. Anyway, our marriage as you know was a flop."

"Well, that's how it turns out very often, Rocky. Nobody to blame."

"I'm sorry we got tangled up in it. Tell you the truth, I realized only later that we were friends, not lovers, as the saying goes. Life sure trips you up, don't it?" Now he spoke ruefully, sadly. "She used to worry that she wouldn't be able to have a baby, with her funny heart and all that. She was right. She lost it. Maybe that would've changed everything." He paused, shaking his head. "How does she look? She was a real looker."

"Well, the men still whistle, I hear."

"She never remarried, heh?"

"Couple of romances, but I guess the right guy never showed."

"She still got that dreamy thing in her head? She loved to daydream. I always thought she coulda been a poet, with some training, I mean."

Donald smiled. "She'd enjoy knowing that."

"Well, give her my best." He rose from the bench. "Listen, I gotta meet a man about a dog. You think I'm kidding? I'm involved in the dog races here, keeps my mind busy, and my buddies are looking over some canines we might want to race. I'm gambling a little, keeps my mind off bad things. Maybe I'll run into you again." He turned, hesitated. "Where did you say she's staying?"

Donald was offhand. "A small place called *Sea Breeze*."

"Stay healthy." He winked and sauntered off, leaving behind a faint odor of hair pomade.

Rocky. The nickname started in school after the kids said he had rocks in his head. He once explained he didn't mind the name even though it made him come off dumb. Rocky wasn't dumb, just a little slow to show his feelings. And he proved himself, he didn't scare off at Fran's illness when he found out, and finally married her. Donald remembered how pretty she was: she was slim, with searching blue eyes and a mouth ready for laughter. She had lots of boyfriends, that is until the heart problem was discovered. She could still do lots of things, go on hikes and picnics, and even dances, but she had to be more careful. She had to come home early from dates. All this made her sad; often he would find her crying in her room, she said it was the blues but Donald knew it was the illness. Nobody knew then it was something you could live with.

When Rocky came into her life, he cheered her up, he kept telling her how great she looked, and took her driving or to the movies as if she wasn't sick at all. But would she have married him if she were in perfect health? Did she truly love him? The question haunted Donald for years as it must have tormented his sister. And, again, what about his mother's role behind the scenes? He could imagine her desperation at wishing to get her frail sickly duckling out of the house and into the arms of a man.

In a flash of memory his sister entered the kitchen where he would do his homework at night, and whispered despairingly: Donnie, I'm trapped, I don't know where to turn.

8.

Fran at first had argued against the picnic, but she had Mother ready and dressed for the event when Donald drove up in a rented car. When he carried the frail and bonneted figure from her room to the street, she protested gaily, "What will the neighbors think?" He replied, "They'll think we're eloping," depositing her gently on the front seat of the car. Father held back but at the last moment slid in next to her, a battered pair of binoculars hung round his neck. Fran, carrying a basket of food, climbed in the back seat. Donald gave the horn several beeps and said, "We're off!"

"How nice, how nice," exclaimed Mother as the car moved along in traffic. She sat on a cushion that allowed her to see everything.

"Are you comfortable?" asked Fran.

"Oh yes. Isn't it sweet of Donnie to take the trouble?"

"I'm sweet when I want to be," said Donald, and to his surprise began to sing.

"Where are we going?" asked Father uneasily. "I don't

like going too far away from the palm trees at the corner. I can always find my way back from there."

"You're with me. Forget about the palm trees."

"I think," spoke Fran coolly, "you might at least say where you're taking us."

"To the alligator pit, honey."

"Is that your idea of a joke?"

"Let's just ride," Mother said. "I love to ride in a car, it doesn't matter where we go. Oh this is wonderful." And she reached over and patted Donald's arm.

"Isn't this the way to the park?"

"You guessed it, sis. A day out of doors. Family reunion in the bosom of nature." He caught her frowning face in the rearview mirror. He was feeling giddy at the prospect of a relaxed afternoon with the folks. Their small apartment, cramped and full of seeping odors, left him mildly depressed; it reminded him of their problems, their way of living, cooped up, waiting to expire. Could he induce them to live otherwise? It seemed a weary and perhaps futile job. Best to forget it on a bright day. Turning to Father, he gave a command: "Ahoy! Up ahead, mate! Get your binoculars set and give me a report on that truck ahead. Can I swing around and pass it?"

Father brought the binoculars to his eyes and fiddled with the adjustment screw. "I don't see a truck."

"You're looking in the wrong end, that's why."

Father turned the binoculars around and laughed. Fran laughed and Donald joined, all three making a noisy chorus while Mother kept interrupting, "What is it? Why are you laughing? Are we going the wrong way?"

Fran wiped her eyes, now tearing. "It's Poppa, he was looking . . . " And laughter choked her again.

"What can he see with one eye?" asked Mother.

"I see the truck now," Father shouted. "Yes, it's very close. Pass him. You can pass him!"

"Hang on," called back Donald, as he swung out into the passing lane with a burst of speed, soon leaving the truck behind. "Very good, Pa. You're my navigator."

"Behave yourself," said Mother tugging at Father's arm, "or we'll take you right back home."

Fran, her laughter gone, was now staring disconsolately out of the window. "My God, look at how people live in those houses. How do they do it?"

"Do what, dear?"

"Live, Momma, live. It's cruel, like animals in a zoo. The world is crazy, that's what I mean."

"Oh yes, people are very strange."

"Living in a zoo isn't good," said Father. "Except they feed you and take care of you."

Donald swung off the highway into a trunk road. "Here we are, kiddies, up ahead, trees, birds, and grass." Suddenly the road curved to a shoreline.

"Look, look!" said Mother, clapping her hands.

"It's a lake." Father sat at attention.

"With boats!"

"Let's go on a boat!"

Fran shook her head. "Oh God, no . . . ."

"I'd like to ride just a little."

Donald was skeptical, "Well, Pa, I'm not sure."

"Oh yes," chirped Mother. "Let's see if he can row a boat."

Fran said, "Why can't we just sit in the shade quietly and eat our basket lunch? I think going on a boat would be too much."

"I want the boat," exclaimed Father.

"The boat, the boat," echoed Mother.

56

Donald hesitated, looked at Fran who shrugged back, and said, "All right, a short boat ride before lunch."

The car parked, they strode to the dock and stepped carefully into a boat while Donald checked in for the oars. Within five minutes he had pushed off from the wooden dock. He rowed out about fifty yards and rested his oars. "Beautiful," he murmured.

"Aren't we out a bit too far?" asked Fran.

Father, in the stern, was sweeping the lake with his binoculars. "I see some birds!"

"As long as you don't see another truck," said Mother.

Donald leisurely began rowing again, when suddenly Mother remarked, "Why don't we sing?"

"Yes," Father unexpectedly chimed in. "Let's sing some old songs."

"You begin, dear." She nodded at him. "You do have a nice voice."

His hand trailing water, Father began a little wordless lullaby that mysteriously shifted into a more robust melodic rhythm. Fran leaned back, her eyes closed with pleasure, although she knew her father was mixing up the songs the way he always did, jumping from one to the other; they were fragments remembered from his childhood. He used to sing them often on the farm when they were little, on winter evenings with snow piled up against the windows and the fireplace roaring softly. How wonderful it all was! He was once a sweet man; sometimes she cast her mother as villain and father as saint; right now, in the peaceful setting, on the sunspangled lake, they seemed neither villain nor saint, but human and beautiful.

Donald, too, listened to the cracked singing as he rowed and was happy about the whole visit. Even seeing Fran wasn't too bad. He vowed to visit the folks more often, and this time he meant to keep the vow. His eye caught Mother who was observing him with a bemused and grateful look. He winked at her. Father, his singing done, leaned over the side to pick a floating leaf.

"That was very nice, Poppa," said Fran. "Only be careful you don't fall out."

"It's not very deep, even if he fell, which he couldn't," countered Donald with some annoyance. "He's perfectly safe."

"Well, people do fall out of boats."

"This is an artificial lake, the water's barely five feet."

Father leaned forward, alert. "Do you remember the lake we had near the farm? You kids used to swim there. In the winter I'd cut the ice into blocks and onto the ice wagon. That sure was a deep lake."

"That place scared me," said Fran with a shiver. "I almost drowned there once."

"Anyone who drowned there," Father went on, "would never be found. They said it had no bottom. The ice in winter was cut to ten-foot blocks and the rest never froze, that's how deep it was."

But Fran was not listening.

They were swimming in bright sunshine and it turned to winter with grey clouds and snowdrifts. The lake began to freeze over swiftly, silently. Before she could get to shore, the ice closed over her, and she was underneath in the darkening water with the fish alongside, trying to find a hole in the ice for escape. Nobody seemed to notice her as she swam just under the ice stretching ahead for miles, waving and shouting. It was getting even darker. She couldn't breathe. Then she saw Donnie on top of the ice, right above her, and she called out in panic . . . Donnie, it's me . . .

"I called out to you, Donnie, and you didn't hear me!"

Donald, startled, lowered the oars. "What? What did you say? Are you all right? "

"You didn't hear . . . " Her voice trailed off. "It was a dream, long ago, I was under the ice, drowning, and you didn't hear me." She stared at him, pale, shaken.

"And Columbia Hill!" Father was now agitated by memory. "I used to drive up the Hill in my Model-T backwards when I was low on gas."

"Why did you do that, were you crazy?" Mother asked.

"Only when I was low on gas. You see, the gas tank in that model was higher than the motor, gravity flow, and by going backwards the gas flowed down to the motor—"

"What's he talking about?" she stuttered. "Who drives a car backwards? I never heard of such a thing. You never did that."

"I did. Are you calling me a liar?"

"Nobody can drive a car backwards up that long Hill."

"I could do it with my eyes shut!"

"And why not while you're asleep?"

"Asleep too." Father pounded his seat. "In those days I could lift a hay wagon."

"Now he's lifting wagons," mumbled the old lady. "If you keep talking that way, I'll shut off my machine."

Fran listened in a kind of dumb resignation, her face flushed, her pulse racing. She stared at them: did they ever love their children? did Momma ever love me? They never met and fell in love, they had an arranged marriage, it was part of a culture which they never questioned. I think if people aren't in love when they marry, they have no love to give to their children, it's just sex for themselves . . . And Poppa taking me over to the next farm to watch our cow get bulled. I was ten years old. I don't know if he did it on purpose or was just stupid. It gave me nightmares for years.

59

The bull mounting the cow, his penis two feet long, at least it seemed to me then, and the cow bellowing like mad, with Poppa and that farmer laughing all the time. That awful bull with his pole, was that what life was about? . . . The way Rocky came at me, his penis like a club. And not a word. If only he had said something, or asked how I felt. But he was silent, his eyes thick and bulging, the bull on top of me, and Poppa with that farmer laughing, making it all a dirty joke . . . When I ran back during the honeymoon, you'd think Momma would help me, I was just a kid. Instead she pushed me back to him, it wouldn't be right, she said. What about not being right for me? For me! . . . .

"Is the farm still there?" It was Father's voice, breaking her reverie.

"What?"

"It's still there, the farm?" Quavering, eager.

"Just the land, Poppa. You remember it all burned down. Nothing was left except the foundation of the main house."

"And the orchards? The apples?"

"Oh yes, the apple trees must still be there. And the apple blossoms coming out each year, I can still see them."

Father exploded. "Her brother set the fire to the house, did you know?"

"It was struck by lightning," Mother turned to him sharply. "Will you stop blaming my brother for everything? God will punish you for that. Shame on you!"

"The grass was always high in the meadow," continued Fran, seemingly unaware of the interruption, "and the stone wall ran into the forest that led to the pond. And the daisies everywhere, a whole field like in my school coloring book, I would bend down to kiss them." Her voice quickened, caught in her racing imagination. It was a fateful turn, linking them all the more securely, binding them

60

when she wished to be unbound. "And that old barn must still be there, part of it anyway, where we used to jump from the top all the way down onto the big piles of hay." Her eyes now shone with a child's pleasure. "That's where Donald pushed me, and once we hid in the hay for an hour before anyone could find us."

Father suddenly stood up. "Let me sit in the middle for awhile." The boat rocked as he took a few steps.

"Get back, Pa." Fran called out, hands gripping the boatrail. "Will you sit down, please? Sit down!"

Father, attempting to turn, stumbled. The boat tilted. Donald reached out his hand. "Hold on to me, Pa."

"What are you doing?" Fran started to her feet in alarm. "Is that what you're trying to do, drown them both?"

As Donald caught Father's arm, he lost his balance, teetered at the edge of his seat, struggled for balance, lost, and splashed overboard into the water. He landed on his feet, the water coming up to his waist. "I hope you're satisfied, dammit!"

Mother was frightened. "Are you standing, Donnie?"

"Yes, Mother. I'm standing."

"It was his fault," said Fran angrily.

"Hand me the line. I'll pull you to shore."

"I can row," proclaimed Father. "I'll bring her in."

"Sure you can, Pop. Fran will keep an eye on Mother."

"How many times did I row across our old lake, remember?" Father slid onto the center seat.

"Good boy," Donald said, happily recalling he had left his fancy jacket in the car. "I'll change out of these pants. Lucky I brought along my swim trunks and T-shirt." He turned the boat around and started wading to shore, pretending not to notice a group of grinning onlookers calling out encouragement.

He lifted himself onto the dock and looked back. Father was yanking at the oars, making a slow circle, while Fran sat nervously in the bow. She gestured and shouted. Mother seemed to have abruptly fallen asleep, her head drooped to her shoulder, leaning against Fran. Donald stood there dripping wet, and marvelled. The family was spooked, he thought, the longer he stayed the nuttier it would get. Now the boat moved into an ellipse as it turned toward land. Donald shook his head and trudged to the parking lot; if the old man missed the dock he was certain to hit the shore.

After a picnic lunch in a small park nearby, Mother dozed against the trunk of a maple, while Father lay on the grass humming to himself. A stream trickled through the area. Fran discovered a flat rock from which she could dangle her feet in the water. Donald sat alongside, his shoes drying on the grass.

"Join me, it's nice and cool," she said.

"Thanks, I've been in the water already," he replied glumly.

"Your shoes will be fine in another half hour."

"Sure, and a couple of sizes smaller. But anything for healthy family adventure!" He leaned back on the grass, grinning up into space.

"How's handsome Andy? I meant to ask. A sweet boy."

"I guess he's in college, at least that's where I send my checks. Presently living with a young lady."

"Unmarried, of course."

"It's the style. We don't communicate too often."

"Bless them both."

He reached over for a spear of grass and chewed on it. "This reminds me when you used to drag me to the park for a painting lesson. I couldn't paint a straight line, let alone pick the right color."

"You were a good sport about it. And I needed company after my last breakup. That was a bad time."

There was a silence. "For awhile you were painting some pretty good things, if you don't mind my saying so."

"I love your saying so, Donnie." His comment had clearly pleased her. "It's a neglected part of my life. I still have a closet full of canvasses in a friend's attic on Long Island."

"Why not get back to it?"

"It's not easy to work in a hotel room."

"What you need is an old-fashioned patron." He turned, leaning over on an elbow. "I still keep one of your water colors, a little seashore thing, over my desk."

"You have that one? I'm glad. I guess I did dozens of those water colors. My analysis didn't last long enough for me to find out what it meant, if anything." She gave a brittle laugh.

Large white clouds, like schools of dolphins, ballooned and danced across the sky. A whirl of birds enveloped a tree, then flew upward with a rush. "They look dumb up there," commented Donald, "but they always seem to know where they're going. It's people who are in a fog."

"Couldn't agree with you more," Fran nodded. "I look around and wonder what's happened for example to me, or even why I'm here. Is it because of that silly old woman sleeping there against a tree? Imagine, coming here to find peace, and finding *them*. And to make things a little crazier, *you* meeting with my ex, the one and only Rocky. It's like a late movie."

"Well, Rocky was quite a type from the beginning."

"He had his points, they were few." She was silent for a moment. "Imagine him winding up here. One thing, he never left a bitter taste in my mouth. We just weren't ready for marriage, not to each other anyway. But Momma had other plans, as you well know."

"She was your mother, what the hell could you do? In those days, mothers were supposed to know best."

She didn't seem to hear him. "Look at them, aren't they cute? It's hard to imagine they were once so strong and active."

"The old man didn't do too badly at the oars."

"He's sort of sweet with that baby tooth. Oh Donnie, why do I love them so much, despite everything. Right now they're so . . . kissable. Ugh!" She laughed, and he joined her, both warmed by the familial mystery. "Isn't it amazing how Poppa remembered the lake near the farm? Just when I'm sure he's senile, he surprises me. That was maybe forty years ago. It was lovely back then, even with the bad things. The hayloft, I can still smell that hay, and milking the cows, and baking—"

"When did you ever bake?"

"I did too! Momma taught me, she was very patient. And the way she sewed my high-school graduation dress, every inch by hand, how did she do it?" A silence. The wind stirred in the trees overhead. "Those trees . . . there were so many around the old farmhouse. You know what's in my head lately? That we all go back there again. I know the house burned down, but there must be a foundation. How much would it take to build on it, maybe just a few rooms for a start? We might find some pots and pans buried in the dirt, who knows what else? Maybe even money. Poppa the miser probably buried some gold there. We could drive up one day and have a look."

Donald listened with astonishment. "But the land no longer belongs to the family. After the fire they sold it."

"Maybe we can buy it back. Can't we try?" Her eyes were shining with some sort of fever. She reached over and

64

gripped his hand. "You'll be a farmer, like Poppa was. And I'll take care of the house. I mean, we once loved it."

"Sure, when we were kids. But now it's . . . just too childish." He tried to leap back in time, past the faint lines around her mouth and eyes, to that lithe figure running through the meadow with him, jumping in the hayloft, splashing in the water of the dam . . .

"Sometimes I ask myself," she continued, "whether you're my brother, because you don't seem to listen. I tried to make it clear so many times that I was in trouble. It's impossible to explain to you. Maybe one day you'll understand, you'll see it, you will see . . ."

Oh Donnie I called out and you didn't hear me. Her image of being locked under the ice. *Something inside me . . . to be heard. I want someone to say it for me . . .* What did she mean? What did she want from him? What could he possibly do for her? How to help her? Speak to whom? To those aged architects of her sorrow seated nearby? He did not know how to confront them—for himself and her—or whether he could unravel the twisted threads that led to an earlier long-forgotten life. It all seemed too remote, a buried corpse of memory, a hopeless riddle.

Father, stumbling, hurried toward them. "Fran, you'd better help her to the bathroom."

She rose with a suppressed moan and crossed over the short distance where Mother was seated. A sharp odor of urine hung upon the air. Mother sat rigidly, biting her lip.

"Francie . . . I can't . . . . help me."

"Now Momma, try not to . . . "

"It's too late. I peed, but just a little."

"I told you, how many times did I tell you, to call me when you have to go!"

"Yes, I know. I try. But it happens so quickly." Her mouth quivered.

"Come, I'll help you to the bathroom." She lifted her gently. "We'll walk slowly. It's not far."

Mother leaned against her. "I've become a little baby, and you're going to change me," she whimpered. "You were once my baby, now I'm your baby."

"Hush, Ma. Lean against me more." Her eyes filled with tears. Her mother's fingers gripped like claws.

9.

Donald had always respected Victor's wisdom, however brusquely offered. As a young man, he learned to value the rough, often obscene witticisms of his uncle which peppered many a family gathering. No event, neither a wedding, funeral, nor holiday reunion, was spared his unsolicited barbs. At one wedding, he characterized the bride as a full body triumphant over half a mind; at a funeral, he proclaimed a just deceased cousin as not being worth the cost of reducing him to ashes; he wondered aloud, at a college graduation party, whether his brother's son was corrupt enough to go into medicine. Despite this amiable abuse, he was always invited to these occasions at the insistence of some member of the family.

And here, after some days in a climate where weather numbed the senses, Victor's company was not only relaxing but necessary. Donald arrived at Victor's address, a high-rise condo just off the ocean. The lobby was thickly carpeted, and walls adorned with standard mediocre lobby art; eternal Muzak seeped through ceilings and wall vents. He dialed the house phone.

"Yes?" Victor, not pausing for a reply, went on, "You may identify yourself or, if a woman, come right up."

"It's Donald."

"Well, come up anyway."

Within minutes, with Muzak at his heels until he arrived at the door, he was inside the modest apartment.

"You look pale, nephew, with a touch of green. Why don't you get some of our free sun?" Victor was his usual cheerful and cynical self.

"Too much on my mind, if you want to know." He eased into a chair.

"Go out and get laid, cheat on your wife, make it a real vacation. I can fix you up. Lots of gorgeous Cuban women, they teach you Spanish at the same time."

Donald shook his head, grinning. "Thing is, I don't need Spanish right now. It's counsel I need. A counselor needing counsel, how about that?"

"Keep talking."

"I checked out a few Homes for the folks. That's enough to depress a schizophrenic."

"You should see the hospitals. At least they treat the oldies very well. Why not? They get close to a hundred bucks a day for each head, government subsidy. They keep 'em alive by hook or crook, mostly crook. If this was a sane society, the doctors would put most of them out of their misery." His face reddened with anger. "Its hypocrisy. They don't care a damn about the patients. Dying is a business, they drag it out as long as possible, suck every dollar they can get from friends, relatives, organizations. Nursing homes, hospitals, the same garbage. That's America, my boy."

"The folks won't go to a Home. When I bring it up, they just sit there and smile."

"All right, how about a drink?" He clattered some glasses

in the small kitchen. "Marge is playing poker somewhere, brings in the rent. What a woman!"

"A small Scotch, Victor, if available."

"Coming up, nephew."

"By the way, Fran said she'd drop by."

"A short visit, fine. I can't take her for long ones. Marge is the only woman I know who can sit quietly and not talk. Amazing woman. The best."

"You mean she's quiet while you talk."

"Exactly. Now, boychick, they won't go, you say. Not just to a Home, but the cemetery also. How to explain it? You can't. You'd have to be old yourself to understand about dying. First, nobody's in a hurry. One more day is a gift. You can suffer, you know the end is close, but you'd just as soon go on Friday instead of Thursday. Life is a habit. So, here's your drink."

Donald took a quick slug. "You're a genius, uncle."

"I wasn't joking about the Cuban girls. There's one close by. How do I know? That's my business." He grinned, a satyr.

"And Fran has me worried as well, in some ways more so."

"Why not let God do the worrying for all of us? He gets well paid for it, counting the collections in all the fancy churches and synagogues." He poured himself some soda, and shook his head. "She's some cookie, that sister of yours. If she listened to me—but she won't listen. I told her to go away, go anywhere, the army, the peace corps. But she's still around, playing nurse."

"She has nowhere to go."

"She needs a new man. Haven't you got some friends she can meet up North?"

"She won't leave Momma. Period."

Victor whistled several shrill bars. "After what happened, her seeing Momma dead when the old girl was only sleeping late, don't try to figure it out."

Donald felt the drink warming him, liberating him. Victor's logic was what he needed. Why look at Homes when the folks were determined to stay put? Father was adamant, more so than ever; Mother was oblivious to the dangers surrounding her; Fran pretended to be in charge of their lives while her own life was adrift. And he, Donald, simply felt outside of it, the visiting tourist.

The downstairs buzzer sounded. Victor responded into the intercom: "If you're a friendly hooker, welcome." He hung up. "It's the Queen, on her way."

"What'll we talk about?"

"Don't worry. She'll find a subject. Women have no trouble talking. Next to screwing, they like to talk."

Donald laughed weakly, and wondered whether Victor was going slightly soft-headed in the land of the sun. Still, he was being spared the usual sex jokes, and felt thankful.

Fran entered, wearing a bright pants suit with matching silk blouse. She was animated, a faint mocking smile upon her lips. "Uncle Victor," she began at once, "did anyone ever tell you you're a sexist?"

"Yes, dear, I hear it all the time. I take it as a compliment."

"Well, it isn't," she replied curtly. "I attribute it to your advanced age."

"Thank you, dear. But I was also a young sexist. Now, would you like a drink?"

She turned to Donald, not answering, and seated herself in a chair near him. "You'll never guess who phoned me the other day." She leaned toward him, her face flushed. "Rocky."

"I had a feeling he'd get in touch with you."

"Well," Victor exclaimed. "Old Number One. What brings him here, the races?"

"He was very sweet, very much like his old self. He was a louse, but he could be sweet. A long, long call. From someone out of the past, it was a welcome voice, I must admit. He's phoning again tonight."

"Better a good ghost than a bad one," said Donald.

"A sexy ghost is best," observed Victor.

"His call cheered me up, that's all I can say. He has those corny jokes, not as bad as Victor, but they make me laugh. I might see him." She added quickly, "But don't tell Momma."

"My jokes," said Victor, "may be old but they're not corny. Some of my friends have gone to their graves laughing at my jokes."

"You mean it killed them, Uncle." She gave him a cutting glance, and continued. "He seemed very curious about my life. He thought we should meet for a drink, imagine!" She giggled nervously. "I mean, dating your ex!"

"That's not so unusual, sis."

"That's just what he said." A pause. "Don't forget we married when we were quite young, and under bad circumstances, but we did have respect for each other. And he has certain qualities, I feel, for my kind of person."

"He also has a wife, if I remember," said Victor.

"I'm only talking of meeting an old beau," she said icily. "I realize he has a wife, and there is no danger of involvement. And I will add, Victor, for your information, he once loved me. I'm the only one he ever really loved."

Don was uneasy at her transformation. Her eyes flashed strangely. And yet, he thought, Rocky could well be a good friend, she needed such a friend. He recalled him as loyal, not one to drop an ailing wife and waltz off with another woman. Fran could well be the gainer, with no one harmed.

71

"Well," said Victor after a pause, a tolerant smile upon his face, "I wish you the best in this new adventure."

"It is not an adventure. That's another male word loaded with sexual connotations."

"I wish you the best, then. In whatever. Will that do it?"

They laughed, relaxed by the drinks. "Where's Marge?" asked Fran.

"Out. My little card sharp is winning the daily groceries. It's better than hustling."

"I'll bet you'd send her on the street if you could."

"Only on weekends. She's still got a cute ass."

"Uncle, you're a case."

"Women's Lib asked for it, well, you got it."

"Whoa," Donald cut in, amused. "We're not here to discuss Marge, though she's worth a discussion. I hope we're here to discuss . . . "

"I know what's next, and let me comment. If it's about my sister, who happens to be your mother, and her husband who happens to be your father—"

"If this is the beginning of one of your jokes, please spare us," Fran spoke sharply.

"You're wrong. I don't see it as a joke at all. I see it as a practical problem for all of us, whether for you and I who are here, or Donald who lives somewhere else. I'll continue. It's nice to see my nephew on a visit, but there's no point in his staying on."

"That's for him to decide, Victor."

"There you go, making an argument out of a fact. Do you want to hear some facts?"

"Not today." She moved unsteadily to the window.

"Well, pretend it's tomorrow. Or next week. Or six months from now."

"I'd prefer not to talk about it."

72

"Good. Then I'll do the talking. There's nothing either of us can do for the folks. They're old, the hospitals are waiting for them, then the funeral homes and cremation."

She spun around, facing him. "What did you say?" She hissed the words. "Cremation?"

"Burial, then. The end. Why are you so shocked? Let's deal with facts."

"Life is more than facts."

"Dying is a fact, my dear niece."

"I read in Readers Digest, dear Uncle, this article, if you want facts . . . listen to me!" Fury welled up inside her. "I read that at least one-tenth of the urban population have mental disorders. Because they think so much of killing and death. It's the same the world over, I mean the way people kill . . . *Not only the way adults kill each other all the time, but the way they kill the children. In the Nazi death chambers they actually burned children. A grown man pushing a child into the flames, or a gas-filled room, and the bomb on Hiroshima with children below playing in the gardens, or feeding their cats, or in school doing lessons. Oh God how can the world go on this way. Man is really an animal, worse than any of the others. A giraffe or lion is more beautiful.* And what do you think your facts add up to? The same thing. Get rid of people, they're old, they're ready. How do you know who's ready? You'd push your own mother into the grave. You're a disgusting man, with your dirty mind and dirty jokes. I don't want to have any-thing to do with you again. You're stupid and senile. You think we'll collapse without you, but we won't!" She walked to the door, went out, and slammed it behind her. They were both silent for a full minute.

"Well, you blew it, Victor."

"Hell with her, she's got birds in her head, it won't be

long, wait and see! There are thousands like her rattling around in this city. The climate shrinks their brains. I'm telling you, Donald, get on a plane. Beat it. I'll let you know if there's a real crisis, not some cockamamie about Mother dying when she's sleeping late. We're getting into booby land. Enough of that shit. Go away and live you life. And no guilt. Leave that for the ones who can afford a head doctor!"

10.

Three or four days had passed, and Donald was beginning to feel the effects of the sun, the sickly scent of over-blooming hibiscus, the omnipotent Venus flytraps in every garden, all blurred into unreality by evening neon. He decided to wait out the week and then return home. This would give him additional time to see the folks; even short visits would, he felt, satisfy them and make up for his long absences.

Now, seated in a bar, he was having a drink, waiting to meet Fran. He had a little surprise for her. He gave no hint of it except inviting her to a special dinner which, he had announced, would include champagne. He knew she lived on a tight budget without alimony. He felt a dull pain sweep over him as he was reminded of the frustrations and disappointments of her riddled life. As the popular song had it, she wasn't very lucky with love.

She walked in, dressed in a cool light outfit, smiling, looking very youthful. She hurried to his table, kissed him lightly on the cheek and sat down, without a trace of carry-over from the rancorous meeting in Victor's apartment.

"Isn't this a great idea! I got all dressed up, if you'll notice. After all, why can't we have champagne and conversation? God knows we have enough to talk about. Remember the old days? We'd talk for hours about everything . . . " She rattled on happily. Donald watched her, amazed at how young she looked, how excited and confident. He remembered the confidence she had given him long ago, how important she had been to him as a boy growing up, and how close he had been to her.

He returned her smile. "OK, we're celebrating tonight. Champagne, the works, anything you want except expensive jewelry." He called for the waiter.

"Our night," Fran said, lifting her empty glass with a flourish. "Brother and sister night."

They drank champagne and ate scampi and laughed and talked of old times, and told stories of Mother's daring and Father's rectitude. After awhile, Donald glanced at his watch. Ten o'clock.

She leaned forward, touched his hand, her eyes bright. "I have something to tell you."

"Good news or bad?"

"Well, I just got an apartment. I've moved out of that awful hotel. Two bedrooms. You must come and see it, soon as we're through with dinner. A little more than I'd want to spend, but I'll manage. Just think—a place of my own!"

"That's great. You should have taken that step long ago." He was happy and relieved at her excitement.

"It'll give me a chance to take stock. You know the old dream of mine, painter in a garret, that sort of thing? Well, this is a lot classier than a garret—"

"Hey, you deserve it, enjoy it. What brought all this on?

It doesn't matter. I never knew why you gave it up a dozen years ago."

"Ten, twelve, twenty . . . Isn't it weird about time and life? My God, the two magazines!" She laughed. "Anyway, I want to forget all that ancient history. It's two lovers gone and no number three in sight. So it's back to the easel. There's a nutty Larry Rivers streak in my work, maybe I'll develop something of my own."

"Bravo to that! I'll buy the first watercolor off the canvas."

"You don't use canvas for watercolors, you Philistine."

"Well, whatever."

"Lawyers and art, ugh." She sat back in her chair and reached into her purse. "And now, I'm giving you a set of keys to the place."

"Keys?"

"For the apartment. Just in case you want to be by yourself when you're here, let your hair down, meditate." She pushed the keys toward him.

"I don't need the keys," Donald said.

"Doesn't every man need a place away from home?"

He looked at her steadily. "I don't know when I'll be back." He was aware at the catch of uncertainty in his voice.

"What's the harm in having a set of keys? Let this be a tiny bit of home for you. We'll take a look at it after dinner, you just have to see it."

"Fran, now listen," he said bluntly. "It won't work, the setup simply isn't right for a number of reasons. I'm just not here enough to . . . " He paused. Was he going to say "to get involved"?

She toyed with the knife on her plate, her eyes avoiding his. "You've changed, Donnie. I should have known better then to expect an ounce of gratitude from you, the smallest courtesy, in view of all the things I did for you—"

Donald interrupted. "I don't know what you're talking about."

"Of course you don't. Ever since you were married to that woman—"

"Why do you say 'that woman' like it's something out of a movie? Can't you say Debbie?"

"She's a snob. You know that, don't you?"

"Only to some people, maybe, and let's get off the subject."

"Ever since you were married," Fran repeated, "you've neglected your family, your parents, and me."

"I'm glad you remember that I have my own family who need my time and attention. So much for neglect."

He was sorry he said that. In fact, the whole evening had suddenly gone sour. Then his eyes looked past her and he smiled with relief. A birthday cake was being wheeled into the room by the waiter, its candles neatly spaced and burning. At that moment two other waiters began to sing Happy Birthday. Fran, startled, turned as the cart approached the table. The song was over, a knife was handed to her as she sat there, slightly dazed.

"Come on, kid, cut the cake. It's your birthday, whether you admit to it or not." He rose, leaned over, and kissed her on the forehead. The waiters applauded as Fran cut several slices, the applause enlarging to the nearby tables.

Her eyes filled with tears. "How did you know?"

"I just knew. I . . . OK, Mother reminded me. But the rest was my own idea!"

"I haven't had a birthday dinner in . . . " Her voice trembled. " . . . Couple of hundred years."

Donald lifted his glass. "Here's to the next hundred."

"Give me one year, just twelve good months for something to happen."

"I give you that. Here's to the best that can happen. And if God is listening, let Him take note."

They clinked glasses. "Forgive me for being grumpy," she said.

"It's your evening. You can be anything you want." And they drank, and sipped wine, forgetting their sharp words, each making a private wish for the future.

11.

Rocky moved through the streets with a jaunty step, humming an old tune "I Wonder Where My Baby Is Tonight." The warm air mingled with a salty offshore tang; he inhaled deeply as he walked. Stopping at a sidewalk store for a pack of cigarettes, he caught his reflection in a weight-machine mirror, and thought: Not bad for a guy at fifty, still got my hair not counting a bald spot which nobody can see, still can get it up, even jog for a couple of miles if I pace myself . . .

On his way again, Rocky smiled, satisfied with himself and with the workings of fate. Not too much of a thinker, he was apt to accept coincidence as casually as he would a traffic ticket. He had embarked on this path with some foreboding. Still, curiosity and a vague sense of loneliness urged him to take this opening step.

The day earlier he had left his name at the switchboard with a message that he'd call again. It was a tactical move that, upon later consideration, pleased him; he did not want to frighten her off, being totally uncertain of her response, and not knowing whether her brother had reported their meeting. Calling back the next day, her voice told him instantly that he was welcome, and this pleased him further. They laughingly made a "date", and here he was on his way to pick her up. Rocky decided to play it loose. If it jelled, that was fine. If not . . . time had cut a large gulf between them, and he was willing to bridge it with a modest friendship. They weren't kids any more, he realized that.

In her apartment, Fran had completed her makeup. She examined her face in the mirror, decided it was too harsh, smeared her face with cold cream and removed the make-up. Then she applied it again, more lightly, carefully, with the faintest hint of eye shadow. What am I fussing about? she wondered. I'm not going to a school prom, and you can do just so much with makeup, and anyway my clothes aren't right, so what am I doing here at the mirror for half an hour? And I got my hair done! She laughed nervously, her mind overcome with a rush of memory. She remembered Rocky as young and attractive, and did not wish to question Donald about his appearance. She imagined him as heavy and bald, then as lean and greying, and wondered about his teeth. He certainly didn't get any smarter, she would bet on that. For an instant she regretted inviting him over. Yet he did phone her, not once but twice, and his voice was cheerful and reasonable. She could use some cheer now. Donald was not going to be of any help, his one idea was to throw the folks into a Home. That was wrong . . . but what was the alternative? Perhaps Rocky could give her an answer, as one who had once been close to her. Possibly he could help, or advise, or simply support her.

Now her makeup was just right. She looked steadily into the mirror. In her mind one thought fastened itself like a burr: that her destiny lay somewhere in the past. His coming was another piece of the puzzle she would one day solve. And that day she felt was coming closer.

She surprised him by being in the lobby as he entered. He took in her appearance at one sweep: the simple blue print dress, neat hairstyle, the pretty face with the slightest heaviness at the jowls, a figure that still looked good, legs and ankles worth a whistle—in short, the toll of age gracefully carried. But age just the same, he thought, moving toward her, relieved that the contact was done. They embraced the way people do on television shows, over-cheerful, without any real emotion.

Rocky drew away from her, shook his head in comic appraisal, "How about that, kid! I guess it's really us, heh? If it's not us, then it's two other people who look like us!" And he laughed nervously.

Fran said, "Don't tell me how long, Rocky, or I'll faint," joining in the laughter. Instantly, she felt something of his old magnetism. He had aged, the slight stoop of his shoulders, a thinning of the flesh around his neck, but his voice was firm and twangy, his eyes alert, and his arms, around her upon greeting, retained a strength she could recall with a shock. Her first love, her only husband, here, a century later . . . "One hundred years! Closer to fifty, yes?"

His eyes flickered in pretended horror. "Closer to thirty. How about calling it twenty-five?"

"That's fine with me."

"You look great. I'd recognize you on the street any day of the week. How are you, Francie?"

"Hanging on."

"That's the human race, kiddo. You hang on or you fall off."

"You look pretty good yourself. Is that the same famous hair lotion?"

Rocky grinned. "Right. Bought a five gallon can when we got married and still haven't used it up. Hey, good to see you again. What the hell, we're both a little older, but we don't scare each other to death, heh?"

"Not yet, anyway. Let's get out in the sun, shall we?"

He held the door open and followed her to the street. As they started walking, she said, "Donald told me he ran into you, so it wasn't the full shock when you phoned. Though I didn't expect your call, frankly."

"Jesus, kid, I *wanted* to call. I mean, we were once married, and I think we parted as friends. Or didn't we? Truth is, I forget."

"You were a perfect shit, that's the truth."

"Boy, you got a great memory. I was?" He looked astonished.

"You didn't know you were, of course. Most men are shits but they go along thinking they're knights in shining armor." She enjoyed this chance to strike at him, though it seemed more like play-acting than real passion. "Anyway, when you're young, everybody's beautiful. So I don't know if I ought to hold it against you now."

Rocky was silent for a moment. "I wasn't the best husband. What was I, twenty? I didn't know my ass from a daisy. I spent half the day looking into the mirror to see how handsome I was. I was kid Rudolph Valentino, remember? My pop eyes. They were corrected by glasses, goodbye Rudolph. And then, I just didn't treat you right, Fran. You were sick, nobody knew how serious, that rheumatic heart. I guess it got better because here you are, looking damn good."

As he talked, easily and confidently, she felt an old

warmth envelop her; it was the comfort of the familiar. How simple it was to be with this man who had caused her such misery! But perhaps the blame rested elsewhere. They were young, practically children; she brought her unhappiness to the marriage; they both had nowhere to go and more or less voyaged out in the world by accident.

" . . . Your mother, when you think back on it, didn't exactly help, aside from pushing you into it. I knew you weren't ready to get married, and I saw her trying to wrap it up, and instead of hitting her in the mouth I went along because I loved you. What the hell did I know about love but I did love you."

The word "love" struck her with a strange force. It was a word that had slowly been eroded from her life and experience with men, and now, hearing it, a nerve long asleep throbbed within her. She uttered a loud involuntary sigh.

Rocky touched her arm. "Are you tired? Would you care to sit on a bench? Or maybe stop in for coffee?"

"No, I'm all right, I was just, like they say in analysis, free-associating. Were you ever analyzed, Rocky?"

"You mean a shrink? Listen, I got enough problems as it is."

She laughed. "A psychiatrist helps you with your problems."

"I know. But I don't like to talk about them with strangers." He was deliciously hopeless, she thought. And his simplicity refreshed her, somehow cut through a dense layer of emotion and fear about herself. He was unafraid, and made her less afraid. "What the hell," he continued, "life is gonna get you by the balls no matter where you turn, so why fight it more than necessary? I figure, if you're breathing, you're ahead of the game." He stopped, lit a

84

cigarette, and crushed the carbon ash of the matchhead
between his fingers after extinguishing it.

"You're still doing that!" she exclaimed.

"Doing what?"

"Crushing the tip of the match."

He grunted happily. "You remember that? My boy scout
training. Never throw away the match unless you're sure
it's out. Or the devil will get you. To forget was worse than
masturbation, according to the scoutmaster."

She pointed to a bench. "Maybe I will rest my feet."

He whisked the seat with his handkerchief. They both
sat.

"Still afraid of germs?" Her voice was not mocking, but
warm.

"You'd be surprised," he said with a wink. "You can't be
too careful."

She closed her eyes, her body fully relaxed. "Are you
living here now, or what?"

"Actually, I'm half retired. My wife likes the climate, I
like the horses. So here we are. I'm a little creaky myself,
but she's the main reason."

"How long are you married? "

"This is my third and longest. Eight years. Lillian, that's
my wife, is a good sport. I feel responsible for her, y'know?"

Fran bit her lip. "You didn't feel so responsible for me."
He shrugged his shoulders and remained silent. "Hey, I
didn't mean that, Rocky. You tried your best. And I was sort
of mixed up too."

"Yeah, well . . ."

"And my mother trapped you."

"Yes and no. I wanted to get married."

"But I didn't." The intensity of her reply surprised her.

"It was that bad, heh?" He smiled sadly. "Believe me, if

I'd've known how to make it better, I would have. I was too stupid."

"Rudolph Valentino," she murmured softly. "You were awfully good looking, you still are. And what a dancer. I loved to dance."

"Me too. We were pretty good on the floor in those days, you and me. All the guys would give you the eye. Didn't we win a waltz contest once?"

"We did. I kept that kewpie doll for years. We won a doll. Wow!" She giggled. "Oh God, it does sound like a hundred years ago."

Rocky tapped her arm gently. "How about a dance some evening at one of the fancy hotels?"

"You and I?"

"I don't mean your mother. How about it?"

She hesitated. "What about your wife?"

"I go to the races, I go to poker games, I got lots of excuses to step out. What the hell, it won't hurt anybody."

She watched a gull rising on the offshore wind, and felt her heart riding up alongside. She said quietly, "I'm willing if you are."

"Great. We'll look a lot better than the real oldies. At least we can see and hear." He laughed raucously, then added, "God will give me a heart attack for that."

"God is dead."

"Yeah, that's what the kids say."

"It's true. He lets wars happen, and children starve. God created the world, then He got tired of it and let it stew in its own juice."

"OK, no God." Rocky nodded briskly. "When shall I come by?"

"Any night that's convenient for you. I'm always around."

"End of the week? I'll phone. We'll leave it that way."

She watched the gulls sweep down to the beach and begin to devour some garbage left near the stone jetty. Their beaks tore at the meat scraps, and Fran turned away, overcome with the ugliness of the world. She rose abruptly. "Let's have that coffee. OK with you?"

"Good idea. I'm thinkin' maybe I should look in on your folks one of these days," said Rocky grinning. "The old lady always liked me. What a flirt!" He took her arm and she felt protected, and shivered with the possibility of happiness.

II.

12.

That night, without warning, Mother fainted, striking her head on the edge of the kitchen sink as she fell. She was rushed unconscious to the hospital. Fran was notified and allowed a brief visit. She hurried down the white-walled corridor, past the silent rooms reserved for the aged, the beds of gnarled and racked bones, of fading sight and sound, the bewilderment of those finally betrayed by their bodies; past the wheelchairs, some self-propelled, some pushed by nurses; overhead, giant television screens chattered at them in a language of idiocy and color, from a world as alien as the moon. These rooms, with decor befitting a bank or advertising agency, seemed the ultimate comment of the inhuman living to the human dying.

She entered a large ward, the beds everywhere filled with old people, silent or talking with visitors. Sunlight poured through the sealed windows. There, in a corner bed, lay Mother, eyes closed, breathing heavily. An intravenous tube was taped to her arm and another tube led into one nostril. A purple swelling on her forehead appeared doubly ominous by contrast with the pale skin.

Fran approached the bed, leaned over, and asked, "Mother, can you hear me?"

The figure stirred. "Doctor?"

"It's me, Fran."

She moved her tongue as if to speak again. Her eyes opened, flickered, and closed. Then she whispered, "You're Francie?"

"Yes, Momma. How are you?"

"I can't . . . breathe. I'm in pain."

"What is it? Where?"

"My nose. My arm."

She hurried out into the hall to the nurse's desk where a uniformed woman was turning the pages of a medical chart. "Excuse me, my mother in bed twenty-four. She can't breathe. I think the tube in her nose needs some adjusting."

"I'll report it to the resident doctor."

"When?"

The nurse replied coolly. "When he comes by on his rounds."

"But she's in pain. Can I go find the doctor?" Fran gripped the edge of the desk, her hands trembling.

"Please be patient. I'll have the nurse look in on her."

"Isn't there another doctor? There must be more than one in this building!"

"If there's any emergency, the nurses on the floor are close. Now you'll have to excuse me." She moved down the hall.

Other nurses and attendants hurried by on their errands. A doctor passed. Fran put out her arm on an impulse and stopped him. "Excuse me. My mother, in bed twenty-four, at the window—"

The doctor glanced into the ward. "Oh yes, admitted an hour ago. Not too encouraging."

"What do you mean?"

"Well, at that age, and her symptoms . . ."

"Isn't there anything—"

"We're doing all we can. The next twelve hours are crucial. And now, you'll have to excuse me."

She found a phone booth in the corridor and called Donald's hotel. He was still out; she left an urgent message. Where was he? Perhaps at Victor's. She dialed the number and Marge answered.

"Donald and Victor went off to the races an hour ago."

"Both of them?"

"Arm in arm. What do they see in each other?" Marge could match her husband with dizzy lines. "After the races, it could be a bar, nightclub, even God forbid, girls. Victor likes Cuban girls. So far he's lived through it."

"Marge, listen, Momma is in the hospital, Beachview General, yes. It could be serious. Please tell him to call in."

"I'll leave a note. They might get in late."

"Just when I need him, where the hell is he?" She cursed.

"I say that all the time about Victor. I hope she pulls through. If I can help, just call. And call me tomorrow, would you, dear? Good news or bad." And she hung up.

Fran walked back, fearful, and leaned aganst the door. Her mother's condition frightened her, the pale, drawn, tight-lipped face—it was almost a death mask. The face she saw that day when looking in at the window! With an effort, she reentered the ward and sat near the bed. Mother opened her eyes as though sensing another presence. She beckoned for Fran to bend closer.

"Where . . . your father?" Her voice barely audible.

"He's home."

"I'm so tired. If I go home, I'll only come back. Speak to Victor . . . his pills . . . steal one for me. A pill . . . to die. You must do this." Her eyes mysteriously flooded with light, and closed.

Lying there so still, could her heart have stopped? Or did Fran imagine it? She broke into a cold sweat, then edged out of the room. She sat on the bench in the hall for an hour, silent, unmoving.

Later, on the street, she uttered the involuntary sigh of those able to move, and walk, and feel the spring of life in their stride. She moved blindly past low white-washed houses and apartment complexes of the poor, crossed boulevards of roaring traffic, then over a small bridge toward a facade of hotels, playground of vacationers. The architecture struggled to suggest exotic and faraway images, with balconies, towers, curving terraces, all blended in a forest of pastels as far as the eye could reach. On their front aprons and interior lobbies, well-dressed men and women sat, stared, chatted, strolled. They came for the sun, the beaches, horse and dog racing; young, middle-aged, or old, their numbers crowded the streets and nightclubs. During the day, the docile air lulled their senses; at night, the neon gave a false idyllic glow. They rarely, if ever, crossed the boundary where their brethren lived in fetid vermin-ridden apartments.

She saw in their faces the blank look of people who believed a change of climate could change their lives. The women particularly offended her, they were groomed for a tawdry carnival, a waste of pearls and silks. She sensed, under their opulence, a kind of despair. Close by, along the ocean-fronting promenade, bathers frolicked, the young chasing each other into the surf, the middle-aged preferring the beach blanket and transistors, the old congregating in small groups absorbed with baskets of food. The latter always seemed to be having a picnic. Their voices and gesticulations enlivened the beach. In the water, too, they

94

huffed and puffed and shouted and floated, their lips and noses creamed like some jungle savages, defiance proclaimed to the very end. These were the ambulatory aged, not yet locked within their rooms or hospitals, enjoying the last seasons of time.

Despite the cool air, she felt her body wet with perspiration. The mention of a death pill upset her most; the shock was in hearing it come from her mother's mouth. "She asked me for it", and her mind reeled with the image. That sudden blaze of light within those fading eyes, that demand! It touched a fear deep inside her, a horror that attracted and repelled. She shook her head as though to dislodge the image, but it persisted.

She walked back to their apartment. Father was seated in the cluttered living room, wearing a clean shirt and his one good suit. Next to him leaned a battered suitcase. "I'm ready," he said.

"What's that?" She pointed to the suitcase, an unexpected anger at her lips.

"If she dies, I can't stay here. The landlord told me I'd have to move. I'm taking some of my old tools with me."

"What are you talking about? You're going . . . where?"

"I don't know." The old man's voice quivered. "Is she going to die?"

"We don't know."

"I was right next to her when she fell. It was all so fast."

"For God's sake, put that valise away! You stay where you are until I tell you what to do. Is that clear?"

"What's going to happen? The landlord doesn't want her back, he says she wets the bed . . ."

Fran fell heavily into a chair. "Oh Poppa," her voice breaking, "I don't know what to do. I only wanted us to be together."

He came toward her, uncertain, reaching out to touch

her shoulder. Suddenly, seated there, she embraced him, sobbing.

"It's all right, Fran. Don't cry. We'll get along." He soothed her, awkwardly caressing her arm. "I'll get you some water." He went to the sink and returned with a filled glass. She gulped the contents.

Her tears ended, she rose, straightened her skirt and hair. "You wait here, Poppa. Don't go wandering off. I'll come by tomorrow. Have you enough food?"

"Yes. I can shop if I need anything," he said doggedly.

"All right. Just be careful."

"If you want some sardines, I can make a sandwich."

"No. But I'll be back."

Evening was now over the city. She walked aimlessly past the hotels lit up for entertainment and, feeling the need for a drink, entered the *Excelsior Arms*. Men and women, tanned and tailored, crowded the lobby. Their faces held the blandness and boredom of the seasonal tourist. She had, some years back, mingled frequently with these guests, hoping for a possibly rewarding friendship with a man, but nothing developed except the usual sexual advances. Gradually she had retreated to the solitude of her small side-street hotel room, going out to the library, a movie, or visiting the folks. Lately, when she would venture into these lobbies or dance floors, it evoked romantic yearnings never fulfilled. Rocky's reappearance fanned these memories. Where was he now? She longed to speak with him, for comfort and support. She needed him now with the whole night ahead, and Donald on the town, and the next day uncertain.

Seated at the bar, after a second Scotch, a revulsion, almost a nausea, overcame her. It's shit, she thought. Then, aloud, she said, "Shit."

A figure seated alongside, striped jacket, shirt open at the throat, chuckled at her remark. "You're wrong, lady. It's Vinnie Duncan. In there, the floor show, the singer. She's terrific. No shit there."

"I wasn't referring to Vinnie Duncan," she replied.

"I've been here every night just to catch her act. This your first time?" He leaned toward her, smiling blandly, middle-aged, rugged looking, with bad teeth. "If you were a Duncan fan you'd be right here next to me night after night."

"I never heard of her. Why should I? Did she paint a picture, or write a beautiful book, or save a child from hunger? She's there to make people forget their misery, and keep them ignorant." Her mind was cloudy, her speech thick.

"She's got great tits, I'll say that for her." He rocked slightly on his chair. "What are you doing here, honey?"

Oh God, another clown, another civilized American rapist, they're everywhere, polluting the air and water, leaving garbage behind them, he's got the face of an ugly animal, and Momma's dying, shouldn't I be there right next to her, the way she was lying there this time I can't be imagining it . . .

". . . View of the ocean right from the balcony . . . "

"What? I'm sorry."

"I was saying, we can go up to my room, relax a bit. How about it? Nice view from the balcony. Great for balling."

"I'll go on one condition."

"That's my girl!" He leered at her.

"When we get to your room, we go right to the balcony. While I strip, you jump."

"Jump? " He regarded her with quizzical interest, and grinned.

97

"And you won't be missed, buster." She got up.

"Lis'n, don' go. I like you. Whatd'ya say we get some burgers down the street. You and me. Come on . . ."

The street seemed odd, ominously silent. Hours had passed. The moon was now closer and threatening; she'd probably had more than two drinks, Fran decided.

In a taxi, head throbbing. Traffic nightmare. Time ticking along with the meter. A wild convergence of cars. The cab coming to a stop.

"Hospital. Here we are, lady."

She looked out of the window at the large white building. "Where are we?"

"You wanted the hospital, lady. We're there. You sure it's the right place?"

She said, after a pause, "My mother's dying."

"I'm sorry to hear that."

"When your parents are alive, you feel safer about things. You can always go back for advice, even if it's wrong advice, did you know? And we need someone to go back to." She stared out into the night.

"Excuse me, the meter's running, lady."

She nodded. "I think it's past visiting hours."

"Yes, it is. I was wondering why you came."

"Would you drive me back to the beach, please?"

They rode with the sky stretching ahead, endless, black. Mother's face danced before her: a Halloween cutout dancing on a stick, a witch, a nun, Mona Lisa, the good fairy, all were Mother, a wild-haired hag covered with wrinkles who scared the kids on the street. Mother who was coming to an end . . . .

On the beach, small groups huddled in the dark, soft conversations, cigarettes with their points of fire, radios humming, the muffled reminder of the surf. Dark pockets of laughter and music, muted and mysterious. She picked her way clumsily to a corner in deep shadow, where she hoped to rest and think through her situation. Shapes on a blanket stirred directly ahead of her, she barely stepped around them: youthful voices, two figures merged into one, oblivious to her, not seeing or caring, a movement, an exhalation, a rustle of garments. A girl's murmured admonition, a boy's low laughter.

Fran hurried past. An ache seized her heart. *I missed it all, none of it happened to me, Momma didn't give me time.* Her body heaved with internal tears that racked and pained. She stumbled on a tuft of sand and sat down, looking at the dark mass of the sea. She wished she could sit there forever, unmoving. Now, all the clamors of the day, the accumulated anguish, seemed to converge upon her. Exhaustion struck her like a club. She fell over on the sand and slept.

She awoke, chilled. A yellow moon was adrift on the horizon. The air was still, the beach empty. She looked at her watch. 4 AM. The first thin light of morning awakened the birds; that same light calmed her. She rose, brushed the sand from her skirt, and started home. Something fateful hung in the air, an intimation of an event yet to happen. At the apartment she undressed and showered. The phone call to the hospital. Should she get some sleep first? Would the news help her to sleep or prevent her from sleeping forever?

The morning light was now strong upon the walls of her room. The reality of the new day was here. Her hand trembled as she dialed the hospital, and braced for the report. A dozen heartbeats later the voice over the phone spoke: "The patient is improved, no longer considered critical."

Improved, alive, she was going to live.

Fran stumbled to the window and looked down at the street below. The traffic flowed. People were hurrying along in all directions as before. The world as before. She began to laugh, a great release surging through her body, and fell upon the bed. "Mother, what are you doing . . . are you playing another trick . . ." Her laughter subsiding, as she dropped into a smiling peaceful slumber.

13.

ather entered the ward and stood quietly at the door, his head turning slowly, his good eye watery and blinking. He finally saw the bed. With a whimper, he half shuffled to her side. She appeared to be asleep.

"Oh God," he muttered. "God, God, God, God . . . " The word repeated like a litany. He sat stiffly on a chair alongside the bed, then leaped up, pacing aimlessly, his voice rising and falling, "God, God, GOD O GOD, God, what's happening, what am I doing, losing my mind."

The nurse came by. "Are you all right, sir?"

"How is she?"

"Your wife?"

"Yes. Is she dying?"

"I don't think so. No."

He gripped her arm. "I don't want her to die. I want you to make her better so she can come home. I want her home. Please send her home as soon as you can."

"Of course. We try to do that in every case."

"Please tell the doctors she must come home," Father stuttered. "I have nobody to talk to. All the food is spoiled in the refrigerator. Do you understand? Let me speak to the doctor."

"The doctor knows all about it, sir. If you want to visit, you'll have to be quiet, sit quietly or wait outside till she wakes up."

"She's not dead?"

"No, no."

"Because I love her."

"She'll be all right." She turned wearily.

"I'll sit here and be quiet." But, as soon as the nurse left the room, he began his chant again. "God, God, Oh God, GOD, dear God, O God . . ."

Suddenly, the figure on the bed spoke: "Who's making all that noise? Please be quiet."

Father jumped to his feet. "It's me. Are you asleep?"

"I was, until you started that nonsense."

"You look better today. Yes, I think so."

She struggled to a half-sitting position. "It's very nice here. They bathe me and feed me."

"I want you to come home."

"Right now they're taking tests about why I fell. Unless you pushed me."

He sat down. "Will you promise to come home after the tests? I don't want you to die here."

"Oh, I see," she attempted to smile. "It's all right if I die at home, so you can watch. Well, I just might decide to die here." She leaned back upon the pillow, her eyes closed, breathing hoarsely.

"Are you in pain, dear?"

"Yes."

"O God, God, God, GOD, God . . ."

"Shut up. You're a baby, do you know that?"

He was silent for a moment. "I want you home. We've been together sixty years, and we should stay together. I'm all mixed up about the shopping. I buy one grapefruit, three eggs, a pint of milk, one breadroll." He paused. "I don't like to eat alone. Don't I bathe you at home? I take care of you. I don't trust the doctors. They experiment on old people, that's a fact. Promise me you'll come home right after the tests."

She turned her head wearily. "All right, if you miss me." She reached over and brushed his hand.

Electrified by the contact, he stood up. "Where's your wheelchair? Is this your chair?"

"Yes."

"Let me give you a little ride. Come, I'll help you on. Where do you want to go? Tell me."

She struggled to sit up again. "Down the hall, and past the window where I can look out over the water. I love the view. Will you do that?"

He slowly drew her body toward the edge of the bed, and with his arm around her shoulder slid her onto the chair. She pulled a thin shawl close to her chin. "Hold on," he said. Then he gripped the rear handles and pushed her carefully down the aisle and out of the ward where he turned down the hall as she directed him.

"Oh," she said, looking up at him. "You're a dear."

The chair went along close to the wall, with Father snaking a path awkwardly. "Are you all right?" he asked.

"Be careful!" She clutched the side handles. "You almost hit that nice Chinese doctor."

Father chuckled. "Let him watch where he's going, ha, ha."

"Please stop at this window. Thank you."

He turned the chair so that they both faced the glittering bay far below. Birds dipped over the water. A jet soared skyward in a long glide from the airport.

She said, "Will you promise if I get better you'll take me up in an airplane?"

"I promise. But where would we go?"

103

"Anywhere. We could go to the North Pole. Or visit cousin Alice, we haven't seen her in years. Or one of her children, Larry or Gretchen or Susie."

Father bristled. "Why do we have to see any of them? They're a nuisance. All they want is chocolate and pennies. No more pennies, it's nickels now. Or dimes. Little thieves, all of them!"

Mother pressed his hand. "I hope you'll leave them something in your will."

He stiffened. "I don't think so."

"Who will you leave your money to?"

"You."

"Dummy. I'll be dead tomorrow."

He coughed and touched her hair with a rough tenderness. "Don't say that. You'll be coming home. I'll come and get you myself."

"How? In this wheelchair?"

"Why not? I'll go slow and stop at all the traffic lights." He laughed soundlessly.

They continued staring out of the windowed area where the outside world, dreamlike, hung like a vast mural.

She said softly, "I'll only be coming back. What am I going home for?"

He shook his head in mild bewilderment. "Because that's where we live."

"I'm tired of living, dear."

Father yanked the chair around, almost spilling her.

"Where are you going?" She cried out in alarm.

"Around the hall. Hang on!"

"Do you want to kill me? Go slow, you fool. Oh, what a fool I married!"

But he wasn't listening, he pushed the chair around the corner with a gleeful laugh, peering from side to side behind the chair for better vision, going right past Victor and Fran without noticing their approach, while they,

104

astonished at the sight, watched them disappear in silence.

"I don't believe it," said Fran, "but it must be them."

Victor grinned. "Let them go. They're lovers, they're having a good time." He shook his head. "The old girl came through again. I keep telling you kids—don't plan for the oldies, here today, could be here tomorrow."

"You don't have to stay on. I'll visit for awhile."

"Go ahead. I saw her, that's enough. She's alive, why sit and talk about it?" He turned to leave. "As long as we met here, I could wait for you in the lobby and drive you back."

"No, thank you."

"Listen, I could be angry at you too. Those were bad names you called me."

"You provoked me, Uncle. You were very rude, if you recall."

"I like to be honest. I never lied to you, sweetie, it's one of the things about old age I enjoy. If I sometimes embarrass you, I'm sorry."

She softened. "All right, Victor. We won't argue today."

"Good. So what if I'm a bad boy? It's in the family." He took her arm. "Come on, let me buy you a drink downstairs. Momma can wait fifteen minutes. She'll be going home in a day or two anyway."

"Well, one drink, no more."

He laughed. "They want to be alone, can't you see that?"

He led her to the elevator. Was he a friend, or an enemy, she wondered? He and Donald both could not understand her problem, some men simply had no depth for understanding when it came to women. But Rocky seemed to be different now, she thought, more mature, even a bit mellowed.

Victor leaned toward her in the elevator, and whispered, "Say, you're looking great. Is it love?"

She smiled, thinking, My God does it show?

14.

"Are you asleep? Do you hear me?"

"What is it now?"

"I forgot to take my new pill. It's in the refrigerator."

"Shall I get it for you?"

"You're a dear."

Father slid from the couch and shuffled to the refrigerator, his slippers flapping. After a moment, he said, "I don't see the pills."

"Next to the can of pineapple juice."

"There are no pills." He slammed the door shut.

She said, "Maybe I put them in the freezer."

He opened the door again. "You're right. And they're all stuck together, frozen. Why did you put them there?" His voice was sharp.

"Bring me some water."

"Let the pills stand for awhile, they'll unstick."

She laughed. "Oh, devil with them. Just bring the water. The pills can wait."

He filled her glass on the endtable. She reached out and

gulped the water greedily. "I'm not sure about those pills anyway. I wouldn't trust the doctors. One of them at the hospital tried to give me a poison pill. I spit it out."

"What are you talking about? It was a sleeping pill he gave you. And I'm sick of keeping track of your pills. We tried different bottles, then separating by color, then by size, then in paper cups. We keep getting them mixed up."

"Did you go to the bank with Donald?"

"I don't want to discuss it."

"Where do you keep your money?"

"Don't worry, there isn't much."

"You promised to tell me years ago."

He groaned loudly. "I told you, when I die you'll get whatever I have."

"I don't want it. I want to know where it is."

"You want to know for your brother," he spat the words at her. "The crooked one."

"He died, I told you." Now she was yelling. "He's dead over five years!"

"Admit he was a crook." Anger boiled within him.

Her voice softened. "I was afraid of my father. We all were. And the money Harry borrowed from your business—"

"He didn't borrow it. He stole it."

She was unperturbed. "He intended only to borrow it, not to steal. My father was behind it."

"Your father was a religious fool. An idiot."

"I ask you to forgive him. For my sake. For his departed soul, may he rest in peace. We're all almost dead, why shouldn't we forgive each other?"

"Well, I might . . ."

"You're sweet when you want to be."

"I forgive your father, not your brother."

"Promise you'll give it more thought, dear."

"All right." He began sharpening his penknife blade on a flat pumice stone, using a slow circular motion.

"I meant to ask you. How old am I? Fran wants to know, for some papers to fill out."

Father paused for a moment. "Let me see . . . eighty-five."

She bristled. "You're a liar. I can't be eighty-five."

"So you're eighty. So you're ninety. Does it matter?"

"Yes, it does. A woman always likes to know her age, even if she won't tell it." She fiddled with her hearing aid. "You must be ninety, dear."

He held up the sharpening stone. "See this little stone? I think I've had it for fifty years, to sharpen knives and small tools. I remember I had it on the farm."

"Oh yes, the farm. How I'd like to go back some day."

"It burned down."

"What?"

"The farm. It burned down. Don't you remember the fire? I told you twenty years ago."

"I guess I forgot."

"Or your hearing aid was turned off."

"I didn't have my hearing aid twenty years ago. I got it ten years ago."

"Ten?"

"When you had your hernia operation. Wasn't it ten?"

"I had two hernia operations."

"The last one."

He nodded thoughtfully, held up the penknife for inspection, and lightly jabbed the sharp end of the blade against his thumb.

"Be careful," Mother said with a wink. "You haven't got much blood."

"I have all the blood a man needs," he replied, now surly.

She smoothed the dress across her lap as her eyes narrowed to catch his gaze. "Mr. Kotlowitz had hot blood, the way he patted my behind."

"Who was Kotlowitz?"

"He delivered the laundry. Long ago."

"I thought Louis Dollinger patted your ass."

"I never said that. You said it."

"So . . . did Kotlowitz give you a little boom-boom too?"

She pursed her lips and laughed softly. "You're jealous."

"Not because you did it, but because you never told me."

"I'm telling you now, idiot."

"I wanted to know *then!* So I could break that Dollinger's head." He brought a fist down on the table.

"Dollinger was very strong. He'd hit you also."

"One blow and he's on the floor! One smash on the head! You forget how powerful I was in those days. Before my hernias." He sat on the rocker and began cleaning his glasses. "I can forgive Dollinger, but this Kotlowitz . . ."

"Why are you cleaning your glasses? You have only one eye."

"Well, I want to see with that one eye. Better one good eye than two dead ears."

"My ears are perfectly fine with my hearing aid. I am hearing very well today."

He snorted and wagged a finger at her. "My theory is that you have no batteries at all, and you hear when you want to hear."

"You may be right," she murmured. "Sometimes I don't know if my machine is on or off, sometimes I hear and sometimes not. And then, why do I have to hear everything?"

"For once we agree. Half of what people say is worthless. Imagine if people all over the world spoke exactly half of

109

what they wanted to speak? Imagine if Mr. Arnold upstairs just said hello to me every morning instead of jabbering on and on about his grandchildren and his money?" Father leaned back in his chair, tired, his eyes closed. "What was Kotlowitz like?"

"I had nothing to do with Kotlowitz. He pinched me, that's all."

"And Dollinger . . . ?" She remained silent. "Well, I'll accept Dollinger, only because he's old, or dead, please God."

Mother let out a weak peal of laughter, then spoke. "You keep thinking about it, don't you? Do you ever think of doing it?"

A silence. Father coughed nervously. "Doing what?"

"You're the one talking about it," she said primly. "The doctor said all my organs are those of a woman of sixty. Heart, liver, kidneys. Sixty!"

"I could do it nicely at sixty."

"And seventy, I remember. Then you lost interest."

"I was afraid of the hernia."

"Liar! You had an operation for the hernia. You just lost interest in me. Well, that was a mistake. Dollinger would still have me today."

Father uttered a wild animal sound. He got up and stomped around the room, kicking at the refrigerator, knocking over a chair, then gulping a glass of water, half of which spilled down his shirt. "Dollinger couldn't get it up at seventy any more than me! I don't care how great he was way back then. If he walked in today, he'd have two canes, with maybe a tin cup, with the palsy, and a hernia as big as a grapefruit. You can have your Mr. Dollinger!"

Her eyes were closed. "I turned off the machine, dear. I don't hear a word you're saying."

"You bitch. You hear every word. You know what you can do with Dollinger. One sneeze and he's buried!"

Donald walked through the streets of small houses and motels on his way to say goodbye to his parents. He did not know if his leaving was wisdom or cowardice; he was aware only of being unable to cope with his parents' future. They could die in their beds one night, unattended, and he could do nothing. More and more these visits disturbed him. He could not, again, free himself of their coming demise. With Mother, it was least difficult; he was freer to come and go in her eyes, possibly it meant that all had been said, they were at peace with each other. He feared nothing from her. In his father's eyes he saw only a distance he could not span. It could be that the old man never had wanted to be married or have children—his jokes often reflected this—and Donald was one more emotional stone around his neck. Like many parents, he was clumsy or incapable of expressing affection and thus very early had shut himself off. Now his age clouded everything, intelligence, emotion, love. As for Frances, she stirred too many memories he had long ago let fade. She knew how to waken old anxieties; he felt better not being near her. She would have to find her own way out of the labyrinth.

He arrived at the *Eden Apartments*. Then, down the dim airless hallway, past those same cooking odors, and through the door. There was no greeting. He had by now become a casual part of their routine, to come and go as he pleased; he was a spectator, while they were the event. Father's manner indicated that the house was a busy place, with life's many problems; they didn't have much time to spare but always time for a word with their son, if he wished for their advice, of course. Otherwise, he had to take what he found when he came by, no time for niceties or formal conversation. It was, in a way, their triumph; they had become more relaxed while he was increasingly weighted with guilts, decisions, futile plannings. The thought again raced through his head: *they don't need me.*

Father, sucking noisily on an orange, looked up as he entered. "You know what she's doing when nobody's around to watch? She drinks wine."

Mother said sweetly, "I've learned to love wine."

"Are you allowed to drink it?" asked Donald.

"Of course not!" shouted Father.

"It helps me get to sleep."

"Yes, and it makes you pee more, please don't forget that!" He stamped his foot. "At first she fooled me, she poured the wine into a glass jar and said it was tea. Mr. Farber from upstairs would bring it to her from the store in a paper bag, and when I went out she turned it into tea. So what does it mean? It means your mother is a drunk, a wino, what do you think of that?" He pointed his finger dramatically at her.

"He looks like that lawyer on TV," chuckled the old lady.

"A souse, a wino, she'll be falling in the street next!"

"Let me speak to your doctor about it," said Donald.

Mother shook her head. "You will not. Because I asked him, and he said a little sip of wine won't hurt me."

"A little sip!" roared Father.

"Especially at bedtime. At that time, so many pains creep over me, and the wine helps. Of course, your father doesn't need anything like that. He's practically a mummy and can't feel a thing. Stick him with a pin, and you get nothing, maybe a tiny bit of blood, if he has any left."

"You be quiet about my blood," Father bristled. "I have

112

as much blood as anyone. And one day if you need some I won't give you any!"

Donald decided to make his exit before the two of them went into their befuddlement act; he was certain they used him to witness their games. He noticed how subtly they picked up their cues for curiosity, anger, scorn—probably this went on even after he left. How else to entertain themselves?

"Mother," he said, "I'm leaving now, on my way to the plane. I want you to take care of each other."

"You're going home?"

"Yes."

"When did you come?"

"Five days ago."

"Was it on vacation?"

He laughed. "No, dear. It was to see you both." He kissed her cheek. "I'll phone you soon, say next week?"

"That would be nice. Yes, you should go home to your family. And say hello to your lovely wife. She sent us such a lovely Christmas card."

Father stirred uneasily. "I'll walk you to the taxi."

"Let him walk you to the bank," said Mother. "Find out once and for all if he has anything in that safe deposit box."

Father grunted. "You'll know when I die."

"But what if I die first, you fool? I'm going to outlive that man just to see what's in the box."

"A little salt, a pinch of pepper," crooned Father. "And maybe a handkerchief, or a mouse's tail—"

"And maybe a little turd you've saved all these years."

"Why not, hey?" The old man was positively gleeful.

Donald ached at the emptiness of their lives and wished he could perform some single act to salvage a meaning for them. As they talked, and argued, and taunted one another

113

with memories, forgotten details, imagined victories or defeats, he wondered at the wisdom of any outside guidance. A final look at his mother—would it be the last?—and, with Father at his heels, he walked down the hallway and into the street. They started slowly toward the taxi stand at the corner.

Father cleared his throat. "I promise I'll speak to the lady at the bank about sending you those forms. I won't forget this time."

Donald knew this was another stall. The old man didn't trust him, it came down to that. The old geezer, half blind, less than half alive, stubbornly resisted common sense. This cagey animal would mess up everything at his death: insurance, inheritance, and money for his wife if indeed money existed. He was crawling into his cave to die, and swallowing his safe deposit key! It was ridiculous, all of it.

"Don't worry about the bank. Just stay alive and well. I'll try and come down again in maybe three months." The last was a lie.

"If I'm still here, son."

"You'll be here. I give you ninety at least."

"Let your mother reach ninety. She'll enjoy it more."

"Not without you. Why not stick around together?"

Father stopped, shrugged his shoulders, his face screwed into a gargoyle expression. The adam's apple of his scrawny neck moved agitatedly, yet his voice was quiet. "I tell you about dying, it's a funny thing. When I had that heart attack some years ago, I was sorry I didn't die. Even now I wonder why I'm alive. It's a mystery to me. Why do I have to wake up every morning? Yet I feel good whenever I open my eyes." He grinned. "My one eye. What's there left for me to look at? The thing I look at most is the sky. I love the color blue. Then sometimes I look at my hand. I move it, I open and close my fingers, I don't know why I enjoy doing

114

that. At night, waiting to fall asleep, I often hope it's my last night of being alive, I pray my heart stops while I'm asleep, they say it's the easiest way. And then, I wake again, in the middle of the night, and wonder how it will be in the morning, whether it's going to rain or not. I don't understand it." He looked up at Donald with genuine curiosity.

"Well, Pa, I guess we all want to keep on living, though nobody knows why."

"The terrible thing, it's my memory. I find it hard to remember the easiest thing. Sometimes I find it hard to remember who you are. I'm afraid sometimes of looking in the mirror one morning and not even know . . ."

"Hey, you're a long way from that."

His chin trembled. "It's all too late. I used to think we'd be together, you and me, on the farm. That you'd stay on and be a farmer. It would have been a good life."

Donald, astonished, stared at him. "On the farm?"

"Yes, we'd be together, you see. We'd have a place right now, me and your mother, if you'd stayed. You promised to."

Was the old man crazy? He didn't remember ever making any promise. All these years, half a lifetime, the father falsely holding against the son a dream of betrayal, the wound of might-have-been. And not a word . . . the hell with it!

"I thought you knew, Poppa, that I was planning to study engineering or law . . ." It was useless now to say anything, to explain; let him keep that dream as an excuse for a failed life. "Listen, we'll talk about it the next time I come down. OK?" He shuddered, his emotion totally short-circuited. "We'll work things out if anything happens, don't you worry." He tried to sound reassuring, but felt the sour taste of evasion. "Tell you what, before I catch my cab, I'll buy you a soda. How about it?"

115

Father was instantly alert. "Vanilla?"

"Any flavor you like."

"Should I go back and tell her? Because if I'm not there, she gets mad at me."

"Let her get mad." Donald grinned.

"Right. Let her scream," echoed Father happily. They started off together. "Promise to come back again soon, will you? Before I forget who you are." His look pierced into Donald. "It could happen, I'm warning you."

They moved out into the avenue, the sunbaked pavement throwing the heat upward into their faces.

"Do you know a good ice-cream place?" asked Donald.

"Yes, and with a sweet girl at the counter. We go down this street one block, then to the right." His energy now flowed, one could see the idea delighted him, but when they reached the end of the block, Father looked to the right, then the left, and shook his head. "I never thought I'd forget the ice-cream place. How about that? Unless they moved it overnight."

Donald laughed. "Come on, Pa, let's just walk until we strike ice-cream, OK?" He put his arm around his father's shoulder as they crossed the street, his fingers stung by contact with the skeletal frame. His flesh is fading, shall I see him alive again? Donald thought. He resisted a powerful desire to lift the old man into his arms and hold him to his breast like a child.

15.

The night sky was filled with flashing stars. Other lights gliding across the windshield indicated to Donald that the airport was not too far distant. As the car drove ahead, he felt more relaxed than he had been any time of his visit. He was glad to be going home. Nothing new had been accomplished, but prior visits had taught him to expect this. At least, he thought with relief, Mother had not been dead upon his arrival, and was very much alive upon his departure. Her recent hospital emergency over, he could go with an easy heart.

He glanced at Fran at the wheel. Her offering to drive him to the airport was a good omen; she was letting him depart without reproach.

"I'm glad Momma came home before you decided to leave," she said.

"I timed it that way, or didn't you guess?" He could see her smile in the darkness.

"I can never be sure with you. But I'll give you the benefit of the doubt."

"Admit it, you love to see me as the bad guy."

"You're not," she added quickly. "Matter of fact, this was a nice visit, all things considered. She gave me a scare, Momma did. But she's having a good recovery."

"Now I want you to get Momma off your mind for awhile, and think of *you*. Knowing how much women in general like a compliment, let me say before I go that you look very good these past few days."

She felt a blush rising to her cheeks. "Thanks. I could use some of that now, even from a brother. You never gave me credit for a lot of things, Donnie."

"I did. You've just forgotten. I said you were witty, well-read, and talented. Maybe not in that order."

She gave a low laugh. "You're not setting me up for something, are you?"

"Not a bit. All I want is to wish you the best down here. Maybe with your new apartment you'll get out on the town, be less of a nurse and more of a gal on the lookout."

She didn't reply, her attention on navigating the traffic lanes into the airport. "Men always think we need them. And you know, we do, like it or not. But I think something good is happening for me, with Rocky . . ."

"Rocky? How do you mean?"

"Well, for example, we went out last night for the first time. An official date, you might say." She giggled nervously. "He took me dancing."

"Talk about reliving the old days—didn't you two win a cup once, or am I wrong?"

"You're right. And it all came back, the rhythms and turns, we even tried the fox-trots and a few waltzes. It seemed as if I never stopped dancing, I mean with all those years in-between. It was wonderful." Her face was flushed. "He's married, but I feel he might welcome a change of circumstance, which perhaps might be right for my situation also. Because I'm so utterly alone here."

118

Donald was surprised at her confiding in him. He asked guardedly, "What change of circumstance?"

"This might seem unusual to you," she went on, her mood now strangely detached, "but I hope to bring up the subject of marriage when I see him again."

"To Rocky?" He thought: could she be mad? and hoped the shock on his face didn't show.

"He hinted a few times that if he weren't married he'd think of asking me. He's still attracted to me."

Donald grinned to cover his disbelief. "Well, dear, he can just be making conversation, the way men do. Be careful you don't jump into an empty swimming pool."

She pulled into the departure area. Her eyes turned cold. "You don't seem to understand the situation. What you don't realize is that you have to meet new situations as they come along. Because being alone is . . . " She stopped the car, the motor continued running. "Have you been listening to me?"

"Yes. But you and Rocky—"

"He's very serious. Remember, he once loved me. And I have no one else."

"Whatever you think."

"You're humoring me. You don't understand, Donnie. You didn't understand it then, and you don't now. So I have to decide by myself." She leaned over and turned the door handle. "You'll miss your flight." Her voice was strange, he thought. Distant. Unforgiving.

Anger rose within him. "What the hell do you mean that I didn't understand it then? As if I could have done anything about it!"

"You'll miss your flight. Go on. I have Rocky now." She reached up and kissed him.

He got his bag, stepped out of the car then closed the door.

"Goodbye, Fran." But she did not respond. Her face had no meaning for him as she drove away.

As the plane rose, so did Donald's spirit free itself from the bonds below. Only now, suspended from earth, did the exhaustion of the week reach him. All the old unanswered questions stayed in the air like an echo, questions that sapped one's energy merely by being asked.

"Damn family," he muttered, gulping his drink. "Damn family," he repeated aloud. Fran, he decided, lured him there every so often to shake up his guilt, as a sediment is shaken in a bottle. Was that the reason for her new apartment, to keep him closer to the parents and, even more disturbing, closer to her, one binding the other, unchanging? *You can spend part of your time right here, Donnie,* with the eagerness of a tenth-grade teacher addressing a class. He shuddered. Hell, he wasn't one of her students. And this Rocky adventure, was she drifting into another fantasy? The guy's a married man, and on the make. What a joke from the beginning . . . the boy she ran away from returns as a man who's going to save her life . . . the past keeps coming up ahead of you didn't she say something like that . . . throwing that up to him because who else was there way back then . . . whom she could trust . . .

. . . Overhearing them because the apartment was small and the doors between rooms generally open . . . *"I'm afraid, Momma,"* and he could tell she was more than that, weary, confused, maybe young was the best word.

"What's to be afraid? The boy wants to marry you. That's no reason to be afraid."

"He doesn't know about my health really."

"You are completely healthy. You have a heart murmur.

120

The doctor said it wouldn't interfere with anything in your life, even having a child."

"Oh God I'm not ready for that."

"Girls think that way but life can change their mind."

"I like Rocky but I'm not sure I love him."

Mother laughed. *"Well, dearie, there's not much difference. When I married your father, it wasn't a question of either. It was a question of where I would live."*

Pushing her out, that was it, hinting she find another place, looking back on it she didn't much want children anyway, then later Fran and he alone in the den.

"I think I'm too young, Donnie."

"Seventeen isn't that young, or is it? Rocky's only twenty."

She laughed a sweet tense laugh. "Wow, both of us added together and we don't add up to forty. I'm too young, you have to make Momma realize that."

"She loves you, sis, and thinks of doing the best for you."

"It's just, Donnie, I'm not ready. I don't want to leave yet. I want to finish school, and maybe college. I have ambition."

Not that Mother wanted to push her out but shed the whole responsiblity, and here was Rocky wanting to take it on, and with the heart murmur it was too much to risk losing him. And what could Donald do about it? Himself getting ready for college, and what could he say about girls getting married, whether they did or didn't and even if she was his sister. It was up to her and Rocky, whether they felt pushed or not, but certainly home wasn't the happiest place for her. And who could figure Mother out anyway? A dinky sort of wedding, only a handful of relatives and friends, and Father showing up at the end as though he were ashamed of the whole business. Everybody liked Rocky with his hair

121

slicked down and a wing collar wherever he picked it up which was old-fashioned but nobody seemed to mind what with the booze and good cheer . . .

She came home the next day and ran into her room without a word, and he could hear her crying, and then their voices . . .

"What do you mean you were afraid?"

"I can't explain it, Momma. I felt faint. I thought something would happen during sex, maybe my heart would stop. I wasn't afraid of him, it was myself, don't you see?"

"Now Fran, this is childish, running home the day after your wedding."

"I have to think it through, the whole thing."

"And leave that nice young man alone, wondering what happened, blaming himself? He must be miserable."

"I'm miserable. Can't you see that, Momma?"

"Go back to him. He'll protect you. He's your husband."

"I can't, Momma."

"You dry your eyes and turn right around and go back!"

Coming to the door he shouted, Leave her alone, Mother, what the hell are you doing, if she doesn't want to be married she doesn't have to be! And Fran rushing to him, crying against him, and Mother raising her eyes in despair . . .

Did he say that or imagine it, so long ago, and wishing then he was a million miles away not being old enough or wise enough to handle such a sitaution . . .

Donald slept, and woke, and stared out of the small window of the plane into the darkness, yearning for the blaze of light below, the city that was home.

16.

When Father awoke one morning he could not
move his head, not to the right or the left. In
panic, he called out, "Something happened to
me!"

Mother was already awake. "What's the matter?"

"My head won't turn."

"Can you stand up?"

Trembling, moving slowly, he rose, stood still for a
moment, then dressed. He had heard of these sudden mysterious ailments, and was frightened. "I'm going to the
hospital for X-rays. I'll take a taxi."

"Yes, that would be best, dear." She walked with him to
the door and kissed him.

He had been to the hospital many times before, twice in
an ambulance, and arriving by taxi gave him a sense of
relative well-being. He remembered his last heart attack
and his surprise at recovery. He had felt he was dying then,
he strongly wished to die, but he awoke with a nurse
bending over him and saying, "You'll be all right now."
Liars! He wouldn't be all right any more, they said that to

all the patients to keep them going until the next attack, or accident. He thought: if they only knew how frightened we are to keep living this way, more frightened than dying. Liars, all of them, living off our tired bodies, getting government money or bleeding our children to keep us here against our wish.

He shuffled to the reception desk, showed his insurance card, and was told to wait. Waiting, now many hours had he waited these past years. Enough hours to sleep for a month or take a trip to the moon. Why weren't there more doctors? If they built one battleship less, he mumbled to himself, they could have a hundred doctors to examine us right away instead of making us sit and wait and worry. He waited two hours for his examination, and was then told he could leave. "What does my X-ray show?" he asked, putting on his shirt.

"We'll let you know soon. It's not very serious."

"Then why take X-rays? I thought X-rays is serious."

The doctor smiled, all doctors smiled the same way. "It's just a precaution. You can turn your head a bit, so I'd guess it's a muscle pull, something like that."

"I told you I didn't know how I got it—"

"You did, Pop."

"Why can't you tell me now about my X-rays? Otherwise I'll worry."

"No need. You let *me* worry. I'm the doctor. You can go home now. Take some aspirin if you're uncomfortable. Some sun won't hurt. Come back in a week if it still hurts."

Father left, muttering, "Who says you're the doctor? Did I see your diploma? You could be the garbage collector for all I know. You take an X-ray, so tell the man what it says. How much do you get paid for not telling me what I have to know so I won't worry? Fakers, all of you!"

The day was warm and sunny. He looked up at the sky

124

and marvelled. Why blue? Why not green? Why not the tree blue and the sky green? There must be a reason for everything, even this accident. Maybe God wants me to be here while she's still alive? Maybe I'm supposed to take care of her. Soon she won't hear a thing, the machine won't help. She can talk to herself, the way I'm doing, it's very nice. People pass you on the street and don't know you're talking to yourself, they think you're just a dummy . . . They see your lips moving and think you're crazy but they're wrong. It's better just to talk to yourself. All my talking to Donald was a mistake, a waste, I'm happy he's gone, I don't need him. She says I love him. Is that possible? It all seems so far away, my feelings for him. What did he want from me at the bank? He thinks my mind is going. And Francie, she's a foxy one, just like her mother. I have to be careful of those two . . . What if I kept walking and didn't go home at all, just walk and walk until someone finds me? Imagine if I didn't show up to help her with her bath? I couldn't do that, no, no . . . I wonder how many times Kotlowitz had her, or was it Dollinger? Maybe others too. But she could be dreaming it all. If it's all turning into a dream, who is she, who am I . . . If I love Donald, that would be beautiful. A father should love his son. If only I could be sure. I'm tired of thinking . . . Should I get some ice-cream from that nice girl at the corner store? She always has a smile for me, she thinks I'm an old man with one eye and that I can't see how pretty she is. But when she wears a low blouse I can look down and see her titties, and my heart gives a little jump the same way it does when I see the blue sky every morning . . . Dear God am I dreaming it all . . .

"Hey, watch out!" A voice from a police car. Father was in the middle of the street. His mind gripped, he turned and hurried to the curb. The police car drove on. Soon he boarded a bus until it passed the little square with the twin palm trees which he recognized as his landmark. He got off at the corner, blinking in the sun.

Moments later, he walked through the door, where Mother greeted him impatiently. "They didn't keep you there?"

"Not if I could walk. X-rays. I must have a thousand X-rays in my file."

"What did the doctor say?"

"He said I was alive." Father laughed giddily. "X-rays show only the bones, did you know that?"

"Forget your X-rays. Francie stopped by and she looked a little funny."

Father stirred some juice in a pitcher. "Looking doesn't mean a thing. The doctor who took my X-rays looked crazy. The question is, is he?"

"What are we going to do?"

"About what?"

"Fran. I feel something different in her lately. Her eyes. There is something in her eyes."

Father stopped, meditated. "Why don't they both leave us alone? We can't help them any more. Don't they understand that?"

"Did Donald go back home?"

"I told you, he left last week. He doesn't realize I can still wheel my shopping cart to the market. He should understand that."

Mother sighed. "He's kind-hearted but he's stingy. He never even brought me a box of candy. Now Francie always brings me little gifts, like perfumed soap for my bath and chocolate mints." A pause, her head bobbing slightly. "She's unhappy. I look into her eyes and see terrible things. I see her suffering. Did you ever think it might help for her to see a doctor?"

"What are you talking about? She's not sick."

126

"I mean for her mind. It's in her mind."

"What's in her mind?"

"Her trouble. You don't see it, but I do. There must be some way to help her."

"How can you help her? She's grown up. She's had one husband and turned down two others."

"She's my lost, lonely child. I won't be happy until she's happy. We're responsible for her bad heart, remember."

"Are you blaming me again?" Father shouted. "Are you saying it's my fault? We gave her all that we could. You're making me sick with all that talk. On and on, for years, whether she's here or runs off somewhere—"

"She has no home, you fool."

"Let her find a home, make a home, am I supposed to worry about that? The way she sits and looks at us, years, years, and won't leave."

"You're a heartless monster," she cried. "I hope a mosquito bites you while you're asleep. One drop from you, and you're finished!"

Father sat in his chair and sulked. Mother seemed to doze for a moment, then asked, "Is it time for my orange?"

"No."

"Then I'll wait. Let me see you turn your neck, dear."

"No."

"Please. I want to see if it works. Turn it."

Father grunted and turned his neck slowly to the right and then to the left. He grimaced. "Are you satisfied?"

"Yes. It turns nicely."

A pause. "Would you like some tea?"

"That would be lovely. With a lump of sugar, please."

17.

"Mrs. Gruber told me her husband wants to be cremated."

Father snorted. "By all means. He looks like a pile of ashes even now."

"I told her we had two burial plots on Long Island, and she said it was old-fashioned," said Mother.

"You can tell her that I want to be in a box when I die. If Mr. Gruber wants to be in a little dish, I don't object."

"Then at least we should think of having the plots changed. There are plenty of cemeteries right here."

"I like the Long Island cemetery. I visited the grounds and I'll feel at home there. Anyway, it's all arranged." Father was polishing his shoes with a folded rag. He did it slowly, laboriously, holding the leather up to the light.

Mother laughed. "You've been polishing those shoes for an hour. Are you going to a ball?"

"They're my only good shoes. I think I bought them . . . wasn't it twenty years ago?"

"Was it twenty? Dear me. Where were we then?"

128

"We were here. Not in this room, but in this city. Yes, I'm sure." He held up the shoe. "Good leather, look at it."

"Are you going to be buried in those shoes?"

"I'm not sure yet. I might decide on slippers. Whatever I decide, it will be written down on paper, complete instructions." He chortled. "That will surprise them all."

"Yes, but what if they put on your other shoes, the tight ones, what then?" Mother clapped her hands in delight. "They'll pinch you!"

Father appeared hurt. "Would they do that?"

"You never know what they'd do to us. They don't like us, the younger ones. They want us dead, and God knows we try to die, but we keep on living. Is that our fault? We can't just stop breathing." Her voice quavered with indignation. "When we got to the hospital, they stuff us with all kinds of medicines. Do we ask them to do that?" She paused, observing Father closely. "Move a little to the light."

Startled, he obeyed. "What's the matter?"

"You look pale. I think you have less blood today than I ever can remember."

He struck the table with his open palm. "Stop that! I told you how much blood you have has nothing to do with how pale you are. They're two different things. Is that clear once and for all? I have as much blood as you do. You keep nagging at me that I haven't any blood. You make me sick!" Father was trembling with anger. His one eye glared into space.

"All right," Mother soothed. "I'm sorry. I thought you looked pale, that's all. How do you feel, dear?"

"I feel perfectly fine, you damn well know I do. I'm in good health, damn all doctors!"

Now Mother laughed. "What if we both live to be a hundred?"

"What? I'll tell you what. The children will go crazy. They can't wait to get my money."

After a pause, she asked, "How much money have you got?"

"Ha, ha. Nobody will know."

"I would like to know. I'll bet you have a hundred dollars."

"You do, eh? Suppose I tell you it's over a thousand. Maybe over five thousand."

"Oh, what a liar you are."

"Maybe ten thousand, ha, ha!" And he laughed in a high pitch.

Mother sighed. "Anyway, dear, about the funeral plot. Do you realize it will cost a hundred dollars at least to send our bodies to those Long Island plots? Is it practical?"

"When you're dead, you don't have to be practical. I don't want to be buried down here with all the doddering creeps. And the climate is better up North."

"Would you be nice enough to talk to Mrs. Gruber?"

"Yes, if she lets me talk. I won't sit there while she drools on for an hour. I'm willing to give her my point of view on burial, if that's what you want."

"You're a darling. And your eye looks better today."

Then the door swung open. In walked Fran and Rocky. Her face flushed, she said, "Guess who I ran into? Would you believe it? And he came along with me to say hello."

Rocky coughed, smiled, wet his lips. "I hope I'm welcome."

Father and Mother peered up at the newcomer. An uneasy silence. Father moved closer. "Say, how about that? It isn't him . . . Is that you, Rocky?"

"Nobody else, Pop."

"Who is it?" Mother asked.

Fran said, "This is Rocky, don't you remember?"

She looked at him, eyes blinking. Some old familiarity stirred within her, a blurred rush of emotion she found difficult to absorb. Yes, it was someone she knew, or had known, or recently met . . . Rocky, hadn't he come to the house once before? She struggled to put him into place, the lines of her brow deepening.

"Well, Momma?"

"I don't remember," replied Mother firmly.

Father chimed in, "Her mind's going. Going, going, gone!"

"I married your daughter, Ma." Rocky grinned, coming forward into the room. "You gave me your blessing."

"You're going to marry my sweet Frances?" Mother asked in a piping voice. They all laughed.

"I did once," said Rocky, with a wink.

"You should, you should!" Mother insisted wildly. It seemed an error of speech; however, her joyful face hinted that it was a jolt of time: she was somehow back some thirty years, observing Rocky with a shrewd but inviting eye. "She's a lovely girl, remember that. You won't find girls like that on street corners, or in puddings."

"Come on, Momma, stop the commercial," exclaimed Fran, enjoying the scene, not at all perturbed by Mother's time flipout.

"You're too young, people will say. Is sixteen too young? I was married at sixteen. To that man standing there. And we've had a perfect marriage, whatever he says."

Rocky had lit a cigarette and appeared utterly relaxed. "Trouble with me, Ma, I'm not sure I want to get married."

"If not today, tomorrow!"

They laughed, as though a bubble of time had exploded at the mention of tomorrow, and they were with the present again.

"Well," continued Mother, "Whatever happened to you,

Rocky? You still look handsome, oh yes. You and Debbie were meant for each other, if ever I saw two people in love it was you two. Then you separated. How do you explain it?"

"How can a man explain a thing like that maybe fifty years later?" asked Father, not too happy with this turn of talk.

"Whoa," grinned Rocky. "Don't make it fifty. More like thirty." He whistled. "That's long enough. Lucky we're all alive."

"We're still here just to spite everybody," said Father.

"But Poppa, we *want* you to be here!" Fran exclaimed, excited by the way things were turning out. Her fears that they would not accept Rocky had worried her, but all was going well. His easy presence in the room, chatting with Mother, seemed to hold together her world.

"Tell you what, Ma, about your question, how do I explain it? I guess I was never good enough for your daughter."

"You hear? You hear?" Mother chanted.

"Cut it out, Rocky. That isn't necessary."

"But it's true. You were better than me. But I tried my best. Maybe I should've tried harder."

"You were a good boy all the same," Mother said sweetly. "And here you are again. And here is Francie. Still a lovely couple."

Father coughed. "Would you like a beer, Rocky? Fruit juice?"

"Thanks, Pa. Some other time maybe, heh? This is just a drop-in."

Mother peered steadily at her visitor. "Is that him? Rocky?"

"Yes, Momma." She laughed. "He lives here now. We met by accident."

132

"Has he got a job?"

Rocky guffawed. "I'm sort of retired, Ma. I work a few days a week, never work more than I have to." He rose awkwardly, glancing at his watch. "Speaking of work, I have some chores. OK, Fran?"

"Yes, of course."

"We have a date Saturday night, correct?"

She nodded. As he started out, Mother said, "Come again. Come for dinner some time."

"Sure thing. If it's pancakes, Ma, keep 'em hot."

"One minute," said Father. "I'll walk to the corner with you. I need some extra beers." They left, chatting down the hall.

Mother said, "He is handsome, that man. Yes, of course, it's Rocky. Oh, I think you'll be happy with him, dear." She spoke the words simply, a matter-of-fact statement. The air in the room was suddenly stilled. Fran sat at the window, her hands clenched against her skirt.

She whispered, "What are you talking about, Momma?"

"Rocky. You and him."

"He's married. It's like meeting an old friend. That's all it is. Be quiet."

Mother stared at her, lips moving in a silent rebuke, tears coming to her eyes.

"Stop crying. If you cry I'm going to run out and never come back!"

"He'll be good to you."

Fran said, wearily, struggling for her own composure, "It happened already, Momma. Do you understand? You'll drive me crazy with such talk. It all happened thirty years ago. Just be quiet. Don't spoil anything, that's all I ask."

18.

After the fourth or fifth dance, Fran was happier than she had been in years. She would expect Rocky to remain the perfect dancer, the surprise came in her ability to bridge the decades and feel again that joy of the body turning with the music. There were brief moments on the floor—too brief and mysterious to contemplate—when she rose on her toes with the lightness of a girl of sixteen. Oh, how her heart ached, and hungered, and longed for . . . what? A stab of remorse. How did it all happen so swiftly? And soon, when she reached her fifties, Momma and Poppa would be past eighty, yes, they'd still be alive . . .

"You're doin' great," Rocky's voice pierced her thoughts as they made their way to the table. "Just like in the old days. It's funny how you never forget some things, like they say. Swimming, dancing, sex."

"And breathing," Fran added. She was high on too many drinks.

Rocky leaned his head back and laughed. "You still got that sense of humor, y'know, kid?" His laugh was open and inviting, no denying how handsome he appeared on the floor, and even now, seated in the semi-darkness, his physical attractiveness astonished her.

"God, Rocky, how'd you manage to stay so handsome?"

"You answered it. God." He basked in her compliment.

"Except your mind hasn't improved."

He continued smiling. "Who said you need a mind to be happy? You did. I never did. That was one of your problems, if you remember."

"I don't remember."

"Our marriage. You were always thinking."

"I wish I could remember about what."

"Everything. Life, death, underfed children in Africa or India, Hitler. You drove me nuts."

Those children . . . did she think of them that far back? What was it that far back about children . . . ? Unhappy, dying, starving children . . . She shuddered.

"Well," she said soberly. "I think less now about those things. Now it's mostly about the folks."

"Think about yourself, kid. Number One."

"How can you say that, Rocky? I'm responsible for them."

"Why? It ain't written in no book that I read. Sure, you want to help, that's only human, but why be stuck down here forever?"

"I don't know how to get out of it." She spoke the words matter-of-factly, but they crashed upon her ears like roaring surf. Without being aware of it, she raised her hands to her ears.

"What's the matter?" asked Rocky.

"I'm hearing things." A half-smile played around her lips. "Time for another drink. Very mild vodka, please. Be right back."

Rocky watched her weaving unsteadily toward the ladies

135

room. Not bad but a little too thin for his taste. His wife was a little too heavy for his taste; he sighed and put it down to fate. Since his accidental reunion with Fran, he groped back often in his mind to try and figure out what had gone wrong with their marriage. She was a good kid, but too emotional for him. "I never knew what the hell she wanted," he muttered. "And even now, I don't mind taking her to dances and the races, but every once in a while she talks about getting married. She knows I'm married already. Maybe she just wants to get laid." He shrugged his shoulders and ordered drinks. When he was a young man, he enjoyed the company of women only if he could ultimately go to bed with them. He couldn't understand it any other way. A man had a hard-on and had to get rid of it, marriage, out of marriage, fancy broad or some cunt, that's the way life was, what the hell else did it all mean? He silently mused over some of his conquests, nothing to brag about, good solid pieces, no brains but fun, waitresses especially, and idle housewives when he worked delivering appliances. He actually recalled once saying to a dowdy housewife, "Would you like to try my appliance?" A couple of times he got bawled out, and once lost his job, what the hell, he never forced anybody, take it or leave it, bam bam thank you Sam . . .

Fran was no spring chicken, he had to admit. Not old but at that point when you could as well take it or leave it and wait for the next piece of bait. He had kissed her a few times, just a peck of the cheek, during the weeks of their new friendship. Of course, it was pleasant being with her. His wife was often bed-ridden and it was nice getting out of the house and being with someone he could talk to. Fran was bright and had a sense of humor, and they were sort of old buddies . . . Jesus, who said life was a bowl of cherries? More like a bowl of garbage. Getting older was no fun, but

136

he could still enjoy life, his health was OK even though his back gave him trouble on some days. But it was down hill all the way, and he knew that. He lived in the sunny land of No Exit. Stiff upper cock, if possible.

Now she returned with fresh makeup, a heavier lipstick than before, he noted. She sat down and began to sip her drink. "I'm a little dizzy, must be getting crocked."

"If you can talk about it, you're still not there," said Rocky. "Maybe you'd like another dance, sweat out the booze."

She leaned forward. "In the ladies room, I was looking in the mirror doing my makeup when I saw Momma's face in the mirror. You know, just a flash, but it scared me."

He grunted. "She's on your mind. Forget it, kid."

"Well, I'm her daughter, and I do resemble her in a way."

"Yeah, but that's spooky." He winked at her. "Did you ever think of checking your glasses?"

"I don't wear glasses, except for reading," she replied icily.

"OK, I meant checking your eyes."

"You're dumb, Rocky." She laughed. "A dum-dum."

He answered cheerily, "I always said I wouldn't win any intelligence contests. You knew that when you married me."

"I wish I knew more than that when I married you."

Rocky looked pained. "Who knows anything when they get married?"

She impulsively reached out and touched his hand. "I didn't know much either. But I was more sensitive. I *felt* more."

Jesus, thought Rocky, she's on the sensitive kick again, I was waiting for that to come up. "We all feel things, kid."

"What did you feel when you married me?" She pressed

him, wanting more than his laconic replies, anger stirring in her.

"I wanted to get married, that's what I felt. I liked you and wanted to marry you."

"You liked me. What about love? Can you say the word love? You and everybody else in the world, you can't feel love. You liked me. Shit. Is that all you can say?" She shoved her glass, spilling some of the drink.

Rocky was perplexed. He said, "Sure I loved you. Would I marry you if I didn't? There wasn't anybody I loved like you."

She said nothing, her lips muttering an inaudible reply. A shadow moved across her mind, a peaceful cloud that blotted out the sun. And Rocky. He bothered her. She felt suddenly helpless. If she married him . . . they could go away together, far away, leave everything, vanish. No one to follow them, or write, or phone. Could she do that?

". . . But if you don't care to, we can always come back another time, say next week."

She saw him again. "Care to what?"

"To dance. Maybe you're tired now. We can take a walk, clear your head, and call it a night. Is that OK?"

"Yes." She wanted to get out of this place. The dancing couples seemed grotesque to her, jiggling their bodies, the women with their breasts revealed and bouncing. "Yes, let's go."

They walked along the ocean promenade. The cool night air soothed her. Her mind arranged itself into nicer thoughts. The moon intrigued her, quieted her. Rocky was silent, and she was grateful for that. She had gabbled too much and probably said some rotten things to him. If only he had read some serious books in his life, Kafka or Schopenhauer, or even Hemingway, so they could talk about profound things. He thought it was some kind of joke,

138

about the children all over the world going hungry, wandering without their parents, unloved. She hated the world because of that, while he probably thought it was all a joke. How could she make him understand it, or was it important enough?

They strolled for more than a mile. She looked at her watch. "I'd better check in, Rocky. I'll be hung over tomorrow for sure."

"Suppose I walk you to your place, then catch a cab."

"Thank you, dear." That word awoke a flutter of memories. Drinking did that. She was a little drunk, she decided.

At the hotel, without either of them noting it, they entered the elevator and rode up together without a word spoken. He waited at the door while she inserted the key, and followed her into the room.

"We could have a nightcap, I guess," she said, as the door closed behind them. "I don't keep the hard stuff. Would you go for a Coke?"

He hesitated. "Well, maybe I'll share a Coke."

"In the box, if you don't mind."

He got the Coke from the refrigerator while she disappeared into an adjoining room, returning after a few moments in a light-colored robe. He had the glasses ready and poured the drink. "I'm still a little high from that vodka," Fran said, seating herself on the sofa.

"Here's to us, separately if not together," he said jovially, dropping beside her.

They touched glasses and drank. "I had a lovely evening."

"Yeah, well, I hope so. For old times sake."

She leaned back and closed her eyes. "Old times, that's all you talk about. Is that all I am to you, old times?"

Rocky wondered what she meant by that remark. Did she want him to make a pass? He put his glass down and slid an

139

arm across the sofa top, touching her shoulder. A deep sigh escaped her. Rocky leaned over and kissed her lips. He felt her body relax, her sigh become a moan; she snuggled closer to him.

"Oh Rocky," she whispered, "I'm scared of so many things. Like that face I think I saw in the mirror."

"Forget it," he muttered. He kissed her again, one arm moving beneath her robe. "Think of yourself, for Christsake." His hand groped for her breast as he drew her gently down on the sofa. She offered no resistance.

"All those children," she moaned. "Where are my children? I planned to have children."

Now his hand moved down to her belly and her hair below. "Take your clothes off," he spoke hoarsely into her ear.

She struggled weakly. "Rocky, I know you love me. It'll be different this time. We're older. We won't make the same mistakes."

"Yeah, sure. Come on, baby . . ."

"When we get married . . . it'll be wonderful." She returned his kisses. "Are you listening to me?"

"Don't spoil it, honey. Let's go." He seized her buttocks.

"You didn't answer me. What are you trying to do?"

Rocky drew her under him. "I'm trying to fuck you, how about some help?"

With a howl of rage, Fran pushed him away and almost sent him sprawling to the floor. "What did you say? Saying that to me, using that language. Get out of here. You came here just to humiliate me. If that's all you want, why don't you pick up a whore on the street, the town is full of them. I'm no whore. You louse. You bastard. Getting me drunk and feeling me up, who do you think I am?"

Rocky stared her dumbly. "Take it easy now, kid. I thought you wanted it."

140

"You haven't changed in thirty years. You haven't an ounce of sensitivity in your body. Just the way you acted when we got married, the same way you came on then, with that big cock of yours, like some kind of bull mounting a cow. I didn't know a thing then, my stupid mother scared me into being a virgin for the right man. For you! What a laugh. How did I let it happen? How did I throw it all away? I needed help, and you tried to rape me. You're disgusting!" She was fuming now, her hair dishevelled, drunk and ugly.

Rocky was on his feet. He straightened his clothes. "You're too much for me, baby. The past, that's all you've been harping on day and night. Screw the past. I didn't promise you anything except my company. If you don't want to ball—"

"Don't you dare use that word!"

"Whatsa matter, you never heard that word before?"

"If you don't leave at once, I'll call the cops."

"Go ahead. I'll say you got me up here for a quickie. And they'll laugh because they can see I'd get a better quickie in a phone booth standing up."

She recoiled, her mouth trembling. "I never want to see you again. Because you're a murderer. You didn't kill any of those children but you could, and some day you will, and I'll laugh when they electrocute you. You have no feeling in your heart, no pity, you dropped the bomb on Hiroshima, and on the Vietnam children, and God will torture you until the end of time!"

Rocky barely heard the last part of her speech, he was out the door, unable to wait for a breath of night air outside.

III.

19.

The idea blossomed in Fran's mind with a sudden radiance. Father and Mother could no longer, she decided, sit before her and wither away; she had to solve, at one stroke, their remaining life. She felt as though she were carrying an intolerable burden that could be carried no longer. There was no one to help her. The night before, in a dream, possibly a nightmare, her mother's hands closed upon her throat; but then, in a reversal, they seemed to be her own hands upon her mother's throat. She awoke in a cold sweat. "I must save them," her mind raced and whispered over and over again.

She wrote a letter to Donald. "I am going to put Poppa and Momma on a plane Friday evening. Please meet them at the airport. I will phone you soon and arrange for all of us to meet, you'll never guess where, at the old farm where we grew up. We spoke about it, remember? Poppa still talks about the farm. He would love to go back there with Momma. Why shouldn't they live out their lives at the place where they knew so much happiness long ago? It may sound impractical, but when you give it some thought you will agree that it will solve our problems. They are quite old, and soon we'll have to put them in a Home whether they like it or not. I couldn't bear that. With my plan, they will end their days in peace, and in surroundings they love. I will drive up with their belongings, I couldn't handle them both on the long trip."

She ended the letter abruptly, folded the page and put it into her purse. She would have to check the flights and arrange other details before mailing it. Having made the decision, she heard herself humming a little song. She had found the answer after so many years and could barely control her elation.

She explained it to them, later that same day of her visit. They were at first puzzled, then entranced with the idea.

"I still have my old box of tools," said Father alertly. "I can do a lot of repairing around the place." His body, stooped over, seemed to straighten with the news.

"That's right, Poppa. It will give you something to occupy your time. Here you just sit around in the sun and do nothing."

"Is the farm still there?" asked Mother, fumbling with her hearing aid.

"The small building near the old pumphouse is there, and we can use it temporarily," replied Fran. "I'll write to Mr. Richards who lives down the road and ask him to turn on the water. We can use gas lamps until we get the electricity opened."

Father said excitedly, "Those gas lamps work even better than electric lights. We used them for years. Did you say Donald will be there too?"

"Yes. The whole family, like it was way back. Wouldn't that be wonderful, Poppa? It will solve everything." There was a silence, fearful and calm.

"Is it near a hospital?" asked Mother. "Suppose I fall again and have to go to a hospital?"

Fran stroked her hair. "You won't need a hospital, Momma. The country life and the fresh air will keep you healthy." She brushed off a sense of foreboding. A restless inner voice told her that she must act.

The next day, like a child with his toys, Father sorted out his tools which had lain scattered in the closet for years. He sharpened the hatchet blade on his stone, as well as his chisels. He packed several pliers, a claw hammer, nail punch, three screw drivers, a level, a hacksaw, plumber threads, and a variety of washers. These items were tokens of a distant life, decades past; as they moved through his hands, a shock of time trembled within him like an ague, imperceptible, fleeting. His mind grasped at possibilities long since discarded. Was this a dream, or a real plan his daughter had salvaged from these wasted years in the land of sunlight? He marveled at Fran's ability, though he mistrusted her. As for Donald, he mistrusted him also, convinced his son's latest visit was a plot to lay hands on his money. He was determined never to share that secret, despite periods of panic as to the money itself, the actual existence and amount. He knew the bank books were in the safe deposit box, he wasn't sure if he had checked the interest or replaced certain sums he had withdrawn through the years to open new accounts in other banks. He had confided to no one that one of these secret though small accounts existed in the name of the old movie star Gary Cooper. An account in that name gave him a sense of identification, a sense of power. Still, it was a game he should confide to someone; his children would be sure to laugh at him if they knew, so he told no one. An old man deserved his little pranks. His money in Gary Cooper's name! And only he knew the amount!

147

He put these thoughts behind him now as he carefully packed a small suitcase for the journey. The evening for departure arrived. He dressed in an old suit long out of style, with vest and a yellowing starched shirt. His brown shoes, highly polished, belonged to another era. Mother regarded him carefully.

"Those shoes," she began. "I didn't like them when you bought them God knows how many years ago, and I don't like them now. They're pointed."

"Well, I like them. They're my dress-up shoes. They're practically new, remember."

"I will say you haven't looked so good since you were married," she said, turning to Fran. "Isn't he handsome? Except for a missing eye."

Father smiled, relaxed. "One's blind, the other's deaf."

"I hear everything you say!"

"Why do you lie then, pretending you're deaf."

"I *am* deaf, you evil man. Only sometimes I can hear even without the batteries. Even the doctor can't explain it."

"Well, I can explain it, and I'm not a doctor."

Fran interrupted, "All right now, both of you, that's enough. Soon as I finish my coffee, I'm driving you to the airport."

"Why can't we all go together?"

"Because it's too long a trip by car. Donald is meeting you when you arrive, and in a few days we'll all meet at the farm. It's much simpler that way."

"Donald isn't here?"

"No, Momma, he left last week. He said goodbye to you, don't you remember? He left you that box of candy."

"He knows we're coming?"

"Yes, Poppa. Believe me, this is the best plan. Now, won't it be nice to be with your son for a few days?"

148

"Oh yes," chuckled Father. "And he'll try to steal my wallet. But I'll fool him. I'm not taking my wallet. I'm carrying my money in my valise, in a secret pocket."

"Give him your money, you stingy man!"

Fran said, "I don't think a valise is safe. Also, Poppa, Donald is not after your money. You have to stop thinking like that."

"He wanted my signature at the bank. He's a thief."

She suddenly wearied of their chatter. They appeared to her at this moment as two animated gargoyles, Punch and Judy figures from her childhood acting out a charade, squealing and gesticulating. She had an insane desire to seize them, one in each hand, and knock their heads together. What if they fell apart, their limbs snapping off, sawdust and rags flying, possibly even blood . . . ? She felt ill, sweat formed upon her forehead. She rose from the chair, her voice commanding and shrill, "All ready, let's go or you'll miss the plane."

Mother asked, "Won't it be dark when we get there?"

"Yes. Donald will meet you."

"Do the airplanes fly when it's dark?"

"Yes, they do."

"How do they do that?"

"They do it by radio, Momma."

"In the dark?"

"Yes." She turned to Father. "Come on. The car is ready."

Father cleared his throat. "Now, I was thinking, suppose I want to come back? Can we have this place?"

"We're not coming back. There is no reason—"

"Well, suppose when I get there—"

"Will you stop worrying? Are you a baby or a man?" She could not hide her annoyance.

149

Father grinned. "It's true. I'm going north?"

Fran had to laugh at his incredulity, a harsh tired laugh. "Yes, if we ever get to the airport."

Father was silent during most of the drive while Mother dozed in the back seat. He looked out of the window apprehensively, huddled low into the contoured cushion. Finally he spoke: "Will she be all right?"

"Momma? Of course. You know her habits, how to take care of her, and help her bathe every day."

"You have to be careful when she's in the tub. You have to watch her. She can fall asleep. I took a walk once and forgot she was in the tub." He continued sheepishly. "I used to have a pretty good memory. Lately I'm not so sure."

Fran smiled. "You're getting old. That's why you'll love being in the country you know and can remember."

"I remember the barn, the big hay barn."

"That's gone, and other buildings. There was a big fire."

"Yes, of course, the fire," he said vaguely.

"We'll visit the dam you built in the woods."

Father hesitated. "The dam?"

"Where we went swimming as kids. You built it, Poppa, and we helped you. Except I forgot just where it is."

He scratched his head. "Can it be there, all those years?"

"Why not? Why can't it be?" she asked excitedly.

"Because things grow over, that stream maybe is dried out where I built up the logs for the dam."

"Well, we can look, can't we?" His disinterest bothered her, because the dam was very important in her memory, and it was memory guiding her back, speaking to her.

"Of course, we can look for it. And it might still be there. It might, yes." He swallowed and shook he head.

Fran thought: He's falling apart. He's going to forget everything just when I have my plans all worked out. The fool is going to spoil everything. I should have gone off with Momma and left him behind. He's going to get to the farm and just stare like an idiot. It would be much easier with him out of the picture. He's a nuisance, worse than she is. And he was always cruel to her the way men everywhere are cruel to women. She had ten abortions. A victim. My poor mother didn't have the pill, or even a diaphragm, how tired she must have been, how she must have tried to avoid him, to push him off her body, to protect herself, my poor sweet dear mother looking to escape, and now this shadow of a man can't remember a thing, not the farm, or the dam, or the awful life he gave her, oh God what are we going to do with him on the farm . . . ?

He was speaking again. "You know, a stream can dry up or change its course, it can just decide to go in another direction, especially after a lot of rain. Yes, I remember that dam, now that you remind me. It made a pretty good bathing place, I seem to recall. Well, if it's gone, we'll build another one."

She was now harboring a cold fury against him. He seemed, in a sudden transformation, to become Rocky. Then she remembered a scene from the Charlie Chaplin movie *The Gold Rush* in which a starving man saw his friend turned into a giant chicken. She started to laugh at the recollection. "You're a chicken, Poppa," she said, laughing, "and we're going to cut you up and have you for dinner!"

Father nodded in doubt and confusion. "A chicken, you say?"

"Like in Charlie Chaplin. In this movie the man was so hungry he was ready to eat anything, even his shoes. And then his friend turns into a big chicken."

"How was that?"

151

"He imagined it, in his mind."

"And he would eat up his friend, you mean, because he was hungry?" Father grinned shyly.

Her headache was returning in waves of pain. I've got to get rid of this man, she thought, he is driving me crazy.

The airport loomed up less than a mile away. She drove into the parking lot, parked the car, and turned to look at the back seat. Mother continued to sleep peacefully. How frail she was, curled like an embryo, a flutter of breath rushing past her lips.

"You better wake her up," Father said nervously.

"I can't," Fran whispered. "She needs her sleep."

"She can sleep on the airplane," he grumbled.

"Why don't you go on alone?" The words leaped from her before she even had the thought, as though it were another part of the plan. "She can drive up with me. Go on. It's OK."

Father shook his head, now fearful. "In the car?"

"She loves riding in a car. And I can handle one of you. It might even be better for Donald, less bother for him at the other end. I can turn in her ticket."

The sudden change of plans disoriented Father. He got out of the car and hesitated. "I should say goodbye to her."

"You'll see her in a few days. Come on." She closed the car door gently. Carrying his small valise in one hand, with the other she seized his arm and hurried him across the traffic lane into the airport building. Down the ramp—she a step ahead of him, holding the sleeve of his jacket—they moved along the concourse to the flight gate. "Wait in this line, Poppa. Have you got your ticket ready?"

He reached into his coat pocket. "Yes, here it is."

"Show it to the man at the gate. He'll call the flight soon. Hold on to your valise, keep it near you. You go into the plane along with the others. Is that clear?"

152

"Yes." He looked at her numbly, his chin began to tremble. "Maybe I ought to go along with her."

"What's the matter now? Do you feel sick?"

"I'm scared to go alone." Then, bravely, "Donald will be there, you say?"

"Yes. I wrote him. Just wait at the gate when you get off the plane. He'll come up to you."

He nodded. "You'll remember about her bath every day? It's very important for her."

She edged away. "Eat something on the plane."

"She likes to suck on an orange in the afternoon."

Fran turned and fled. She could no longer bear to see his face. She had to get back to the car, fearful that she had closed all the windows and left Mother to suffocate. "Momma dear," she moaned, racing down the concourse, weaving between the people thronging in every direction. She passed a large mailbox, something flicked in her mind. She must mail the letter to Donald without delay, because it would be unfair not to give him notice of Poppa's arrival. At least a full day.

20.

The following morning, after an early breakfast, Fran closed the car trunk tightly on the jammed valises, cartons, and assorted household articles. Nearby, Mother was seated on a beach chair in the sun, half asleep, her head nodding gently to one side; from her ear a thin loop of colored cord fell across the shoulder to disappear in the pocket of her cotton dress. While packing she had discovered in a bottom drawer an unused hearing aid complete with batteries; she decided to wear it on the trip, not realizing, or not caring, that the batteries were dead.

Fran straightened out the interior of the car. All was in readiness. She paused for a breath or two, to wipe the perspiration from her brow, for the morning was beginning to heat the air; great pilings of cloud filled the sky, soon to spread out thinly and bring on a humidity that never failed to depress her. Now, observing her mother, her heart was overwhelmed by a mysterious tenderness surmounting the conflict of emotions which so exhausted her during the past weeks. Tears dimmed her eyes. Yes, she was going to save her mother at last; this frail creature would never suffer the indignity of a nursing home, tended by strangers. All her sufferings would be lifted soon; from the half-sleep of dying she would waken in a familiar place and live out her remaining years peacefully. Of course there were things to be done with the farm—purchasing the land, putting up a winter house—but first they had to gather there, each member of the family, to fulfill a mystery.

She crossed the patio toward Mother and pressed her hand. "Wake up, dear. We're ready to start."

"We're there already?"

"No, we're starting out. We're beginning the trip."

"In the same car?"

"That's right, Momma."

Her face lit up in a soft smile, made slightly comical by her missing bottom plate. "I'm happy we're going. I love to ride in cars."

"Where's your teeth, Momma?"

"What? Let me turn up my machine."

"Your bottom teeth."

"Aren't they in my mouth?"

"No, only the top teeth."

"Dear me, where did I put them? They must be in the sink. Help me inside, I want to pee before we leave."

The dental plate was on the sink, and Mother promptly slapped it into her mouth. Sitting on the toilet bowl, she said, "He always helped me on and off the toilet, your father did. He's a gentleman. I miss him already."

"We'll see him in a few days."

"You know, he still thinks I let Kotlowitz sleep with me. Well, if he likes to think so, let him. I don't even remember Kotlowitz anymore, though Mr. Dollinger stays in my mind. I don't know why exactly."

"Hurry, Mother. I want to get on the road before the heat."

"You promised I'd have my bath."

"Yes, tonight. In the motel, after the day's drive."

"Does Donald know we're coming?"

"I wrote him, yes. Are you through?"

"It takes a bit longer at my age. Your father was very patient with me. I wish he was here with me right now."

If she doesn't stop jabbering, thought Fran, I'm going to push her right into the toilet and flush her away. Or flush her down the bath drain. She's thin enough, I'll bet her bones are soft as mush, but then they say old people are strong, they just won't die, they hang on, the hospitals are full of them, stuck with needles, tubes down their throats, tubes in their veins, they keep on living just to spite us, to torture us, it's their revenge I guess because they did so much for us. Then again, what did they do? Give us life. We didn't ask for life. They were like cows in the pasture, and the bulls put their thing into them and started life, and nobody asked us if we wanted to be born but we had to be born because of the stupid bull and the stupider cow, both dumb animals like humans, fucking all the time, touching each other and fucking. Why didn't Mother fight him? Why didn't she take a knife to bed with her and when he put his own knife into her why didn't she stick it to him? So I wouldn't have to be born, do you hear, Momma? So I wouldn't be. To be. Not to be. I didn't want it, Momma!

"Why didn't you, Momma?" Her voice startled her.

"Didn't what?"

"Use the knife?" It was casual, soft, conversational.

"You mean to cut my orange?"

She exploded with laughter. "Yes, darling. The orange!"

Mother emerged from the bathroom. "I'm ready." She looked around. "Are you sure we're doing the right thing?"

"We are. We are!" replied Fran. "Come, we'll walk right out the door and into the car and not turn around once." She offered her arm.

"Not turn around once," echoed Mother.

156

21.

Father had never in his life observed the magical sight from the plane window: the city below as a field of twinkling points, a sky turned upside down with its stars. He could see, as this great machine descended through strips of cottony cloud, the streets and highways blinking with neon, even tiny automobiles moving about. He was speechless, his mind whirled with delight. Down they glided, a lane of light opened before them, soon he felt a bump and knew the plane had landed. It bounded ahead for a little while, then came to a stop. He could not wait to tell Donald how exciting the adventure was! He sat in his seat until all the passengers departed; his legs seemed drained of strength.

A stewardess leaned over him. "Trouble with your seat belt? Here, let me help you." She unhooked the belt with a quick motion, and helped him rise. He looked up at a youthful smiling face. "Are you all right, sir?"

"Yes, thank you. This is my first time in an airplane."

She reached under his seat for the small valise that protruded. "Is this all your luggage, sir?"

He nodded and clutched the bag. He had almost forgotten it. The stewardess held his arm and led him down the aisle to the plane exit. "This way, sir. Watch your step. I hope you enjoyed your flight and fly with us again on your next trip."

"My son is meeting me here," Father said.

"You walk through those gates and into the waiting room. I'm sure he'll be there. If not, go straight along past security. He'll surely be there."

He did as directed and followed the surge of people along the concourse until it seemed as if he was back where he started, it all looked the same: bright, clean, humming with voices. He felt a slight chill and drew his thin coat closer around his body. He passed the security check where a larger throng waited. He looked around but did not see Donald anywhere. The area led into a larger kind of waiting room; entering it, he walked slowly past the chairs and benches, scanning the faces around him. His son was not among them.

He sat in one of the chairs. The events of the day had been too new and tumultuous for him to carefully separate and examine. Did he forget any directions? Was he to phone anywhere? No, he had only to wait until Donald arrived. Donald was late. Donald knew he was coming, Fran took care of that. He went over it again: Fran said she had written to Donald, who would meet him here; there was nothing more for him to do. And then (his mind sputtered) they would all meet at the farm somehow. Donald knew where it was, of course, unless the old roads were gone. The new big highways could go right by the farm without anyone recognizing it; the thought alarmed him; they would all have to be on guard during the trip.

He dozed for awhile. On waking, he noticed most of the people had gone. The lights, dry and bright, were still on.

His one eye caught an overhead clock: it was midnight! He had slept for more than two hours. Donald might have been here and left. But surely Donald would have looked in the waiting room and seen him. He would have to think about it. He sat motionless for many minutes. He thought carefully about what to do next; his mind dimmed, weakened, grew heavy and light, and finally went blank.

"Hey, Pop!" A porter was at his side. "You OK?"

Father pulled his jacket close. "Yes, thank you."

"You been sittin' here for hours, I noticed."

"Yes. I'm waiting for my son. He's meeting me."

"You sure this is the place? What flight you come off?"

"From that door. Ten o'clock flight. I'm supposed to wait."

The porter nodded. "Yep. This is the right place. You take it easy, man." He walked away, whistling.

Father sat awhile longer, then rose and walked down the connecting corridor into a large area with airline counters on one side and stores on the other. A continual stream of travelers moved in every direction. He stood at one corner, amazed, fearful; never had he been in the midst of such commotion. And it was in the middle of the night! He began to walk again, edging toward the store windows brightly lit. Books, valises, clothes, toys, candies, and an endless variety of things to buy. He looked into one window featuring a large assortment of cutlery: knives, clippers, scissors. He observed the knives closely, several lay with the blades open and he noted the fine edges; he had kept several of his own knives carefully sharpened and honed for fifty, maybe sixty years, and appreciated the quality of those shining specimens in the window.

He felt hungry and stopped a woman in a flight uniform. "If you'll excuse me, miss, is there a restaurant . . . ?"

"Yes, keep on walking through the arcade, you'll see it,

more of a coffee shop at this hour. Wait a minute, after midnight, I'm afraid it's closed."

"Thank you."

She hesitated, struck by his ashen color. "Are you lost?"

"No. I'm waiting for my son. He should be here very soon."

"You'll find some coffee machines downstairs. Take that escalator. Be careful how you step." And she left him.

An image leaped to his mind. In the store window. The valise! He looked down at each hand, each was empty. A weak spasm went through him as he shuffled down the long corridor back to the waiting room. His glance swept along the chairs and benches. His valise had vanished. Lucky he had put his money into his wallet. He sat down again. He ummoned strength to his mind, but felt nothing. Even the name Donald seemed distant.

22.

Mother kept the window of the car door open for hours, and dreamed with the wind rushing past her ears. Was this really happening? her mind asked. Yes, with the miles fading behind, the lovely sunshine overhead, and in a day or two her son and husband would join them. She cast an occasional admiring glance at her daughter. Everything had worked well so far, and she was happy. She was old, true, and often had dizzy spells, but here she was in a car feeling perfectly well, the car swayed gently like a boat, and all the houses and fields she could see! Francie had arranged all this, the poor girl with all her troubles had worked everything out. And where was Rocky? Why did that turn out so badly? He was a nice man, and a husband; every girl needed a husband.

"How do you feel, Momma?"

"Fine, dear. I love to ride in a car."

"Are you hungry?"

"I miss my orange."

"We'll have a big juicy orange along with dinner."

Mother nodded, and suddenly reached over and squeezed her daughter's arm. "Let's just ride and ride, and not stop!" She giggled and closed her eyes, leaning back in the seat.

"In a little while we'll stop for the night, Momma. Then, tomorrow, we'll get an early start and reach the farm by late afternoon." Fran smiled reassuringly.

"Why didn't Rocky come along with us?"

Fran didn't answer. Her hand tightened on the wheel.

Mother went on, "He's your husband, isn't he?"

"He isn't. Why do you say that?"

"You were going to get married—"

"We *were* married, long ago. We separated. That was long ago."

Mother made a clicking noise with her teeth. "He'll come back, if you encourage him."

"Shut up, Mother." The words were out of her mouth before she realized it. "If you say one more word I'll open the car door and kick you out. I'm sick of your pushing him onto me. You did it once before and you're doing it again. Who is he anyway? You don't care, you wouldn't care if I married a chimpanzee, or a total idiot. He's a bull with a big thing, and you threw him at me. You didn't give a damn what happened to me, even though you knew I was ill. And now you're throwing me at him as if nothing happened." Her voice rose over the sound of the motor, her face contorted. "I'll kill you if you don't shut up!"

Mother sat stunned, afraid to reply. The landscape seemed to darken to her eyes. She shrank into her seat. "I'm sorry," she whimpered.

"All right, Momma," Fran replied softly. "I just want you to forget Rocky, nce and for all."

"I want to go back."

"We're not going back. Just be quiet and enjoy the ride.

Now, you see, I lost my temper. You make me do this so often."

"You shouldn't talk that way to your mother."

She broke into a shrill laugh. "Why not? You're not God. You tried to be God all your life, arranging things. You know who else tried to be God? Donald. Oh, he's very clever, but I see through him. Anyway, he's sick. Did you know that? He's dying of cancer."

"Donald?" Mother gasped.

"Yes. I didn't want to tell you."

Mother felt her head whirling. "You're lying. He never told me that."

"Ask him when you see him."

"Yes, I will. I certainly will. Oh, you're going to make me cry!"

Fran changed the subject abruptly. "I think it's going to rain. I don't like driving when it rains."

"Is he very sick?"

"Well, if he dies, it would balance things, Momma, don't you see?" She spoke calmly, reasonably. "Because so many children die every day, from war and starvation, all over the world. Grownups kill them. Yes, people like Donald and Poppa and all those people who think only of themselves. That's why so many of them get cancer. God is punishing them. That's why if Donald dies, he's paying for all the misery of the children. In the war, Momma, children were burned with fire that came down from airplanes, napalm they called it, and if you saw the pictures in the newspapers, you would hope Donald dies for his sins."

Mother listened with growing confusion. She had never heard that kind of talk before. What did it mean? Why must Donald die, who surely did nothing to hurt little children? She glanced at her daughter with suspicion. "You hate everybody, don't you?"

163

Fran chuckled gleefully. "But I love you, Momma. I'm doing this for you, the whole trip. Of course, Poppa and Donald are part of it, but you're the main reason. I want to save you, Momma."

"From what?" Mother whispered.

"From him."

"Him?"

"Father, the big bull. He hurt you. I'm going to be with you now, to protect you. I didn't mean to yell at you before, Momma. It's just that you got me angry mentioning Rocky. Let's make up, shall we? Please?" She looked at Mother, a quick despairing look, then turned her eyes once again upon the road. "We'll ride another half-hour, then find a motel. I must get some rest. Every bone in me is tired. And my headache is back."

She picked a motel, *Hilly Acres*, as darkness came on. Mother had been dozing again, and Fran did not waken her until after she had signed them in for the night. She decided to leave most of the luggage in the car so as not to delay her planned early morning departure. Nothing must go wrong with her plan.

Mother was unusually alert after her nap, her mind free of fear after the harsh argument with Fran earlier in the afternoon. She examined the motel room with great interest, trying the bed lights and water taps in the bathroom.

"Look at the lovely pink bathtub," she exclaimed. "How do they make them pink?"

"They come in all colors, Momma. Yellow and green and every color you can think of."

"I never took a bath in a colored tub. It was always white. I think I'll enjoy a bath tonight in a pink tub."

Fran was turning back the sheets on the bed. "Should we skip your bath tonight? You look very tired."

"I'm not tired at all. I am not."

"Yes, you are. You can skip a day, can't you?"

Mother pouted. "But your father always—"

"Take your teeth out and get into bed," she interrupted, a strange weariness enveloping her body. She wanted sleep desperately.

"Well, then," demanded Mother, "at least give me my orange. I always suck on an orange before I go to bed."

Fran took an orange out of a paper bag and proceeded to peel it, then broke it along the seams into slices.

"Doctor Libby at the clinic said I have the organs of a sixty-year-old woman, and I'm eighty, imagine that, dear."

"Go to bed, Momma."

"It's because I have my orange every day. I got your father to eat an orange or grapefruit with me, but he often will forget. He's always soaking his roll into the coffee and mushing it down. Well, he has only one tooth top and bottom while I have these store teeth which Doctor Libby can't understand how they fit so well, but then he can't understand how at my age all my organs are so healthy."

"Except your mind," Fran said curtly.

"My mind?"

"Poppa's is worse, but yours isn't much either."

"Why do you say that?" Her voice trembled.

"Because you can't remember anything five minutes after it happened. It goes through your head like water through a strainer. Now let's not keep on talking. I want you in bed and asleep in five minutes."

"I have to go to the bathroom."

"Come on, I'll help you."

"I think I made a little in my drawers."

"Why did you do that? No wonder I smelled you in the car. Why didn't you ask me to stop. You fool!" She was screaming now.

"You yelled at me. I was afraid to ask." She began to cry.

165

"Stop crying, Momma."

"You hate me so much. I can feel it."

"No. It's just that I'm so tired. I'm ready to drop. And I have so many problems on my mind, if you only knew. That's why I yell. Right now, for example, my head seems to be squeezed between two blocks of wood. Now, at your age, what I said before, your mind has to be dried up. It doesn't mean you can't enjoy things. That's why we're going to the farm, to enjoy what's left of life, don't you understand?"

Mother had meanwhile made her own way to the bathroom and seated herself on the bowl. "I'll just wash myself a bit and take my bath tomorrow," she spoke to herself, relaxed now, clinging to the towel rod as she urinated.

Fran sat on her bed and stared at the wall. Mother's voice seemed to come from a vast distance, receding, and finally vanished. A stillness pervaded her deepest consciousness, and for an instant she lost her sense of place entirely, existing as a filament of thought, something (someone) outside of herself. She had broken through a vast space, and more space lay ahead, and still more, yet all was motionless. Then, charging toward her, the figure of a bull, its huge penis swinging like a pendulum, the face human, teeth bared . . .

"Momma!" Her cry shattered the absolute quiet.

"I'm ready, help me off," a voice reached her.

"What?" She rose from the bed, listening.

"I'm ready. Didn't you hear me call?"

She stumbled to the bathroom, and said thickly, "No, I didn't hear you, Momma."

"I shouted for you. I got dizzy and almost fell. Here, take my arm."

Fran helped her off the toilet and across the room to her bed. Mother was quite docile and allowed herself to be helped between the clean sheets. She murmured sleepily, "I miss my old room."

"Goodnight," Fran said, embracing her.

"Let's go home tomorrow."

"But we are going home, the home of long ago, Momma."

"I don't mean that. I mean the house we left. And I want Poppa back there too. I don't want you or Donald, only Poppa." Her voice trailed off, she began a low regular breathing, and was asleep.

Fran drew the blanket up across her shoulder. She took the half dozen steps to her own bed and sprawled upon it, face down. A thought trickled through her mind: she must remember to mail the letter to Donald the very next morning. She tossed, drifted, seemed to sleep . . .

She was turning and turning in an endless sky, then the edge of a forest formed, and walking toward it she awoke. Her eyes stared open into the darkness. With a clarity of mind she had not known for days, she pulled together all the strands of her planning. She rose quietly in the dark and dressed. Standing near the window, she brushed her hair with quick strokes, then picked up her carrying bag and stepped out into the small courtyard. She walked past the edge of the building where the car was parked, deciding to wash and brush her teeth at a gas station while the car was being serviced. She had to hurry, and already regretted having spent part of the night in a motel instead of driving straight through. She wanted to get to the farm before nightfall of the new day; that was necessary in order to meet her schedule with Donald.

She drove to the gas station just down the highway as the faint sign of light pulsed in the Eastern sky. Inside the ladies room, the mirror surprised her with the serenity of her face.

Pale, yes, but a peaceful reflection. She stared in silence and in quiet admiration. It was coming true, a release from her torment; her body softened, even her walk was lighter, she thought.

Returning to the car, she experienced a throb of anxiety about the arrangements. She drove away from the station, and for the first hour her mind went over the planning, every step and detail. Something abruptly clouded inside her head, a disorientation of time and place: wasn't this the day she usually went to visit the folks? Then how to account for this unfamiliar terrain? The highway, the long valley ahead, the wooded border stretching for miles. Her breathing tightened. What was she doing here? A mistake had occurred, she'd better hurry back to the city. With a joyful sigh she realized she was on her way elsewhere, that they were all to meet later at the farm. Of course. The old homestead. Didn't she take care of everything? She laughed softly. Donald probably thought when he got her letter that putting Poppa and Momma on the plane was not very wise. She wished she could see his face (he never gave her credit for such things) when they came off the plane! Donald always thought she was not as smart as he; well, this little surprise would show him. (What delighted her most was the swiftness of her decision.) "Did you think, dear brother, I'd ever send them to a Home?" She spoke clearly, relishing the sound of her voice. "You wanted that, so you could forget about them. I know you well. Out of sight, out of mind, that's your philosophy. You managed to stay away all these years, oh yes a short visit twice a year, a holiday weekend, but you left me to be near them. I was left to deal with their problems, to care for them, visit them, clean up their garbage. But I didn't let it poison my feelings for my mother and father. I watched them grow old and suffer, and how many times we'd sing old songs together, while you were leading your own selfish life somewhere, safe and far away. But I forgive you. I can do that. I'm big enough to do that. Do you hear me, Donald? Oh I wish you could hear me speaking now! Nobody hears me!" She almost choked with elation. She vowed to repeat these thoughts when she met Donald again. No, she would say nothing, there was a victory in silence. She would triumph over them all in silence. She would smile and say nothing.

23.

ather awoke with an aching stiffness in his bones. He lay curled up on the bench of the waiting room, the coat which had covered him earlier in the night now upon the floor. It was early morning, and the airport traffic had quickened to the heavier daytime flow. Above him, the television screens flashed an unending soundless printout of flight arrivals and departures.

With some difficulty, he sat up. His arms and legs responded to massage, and soon he felt the circulation restored. His eye stared out weakly at the flow of people past him and around him. His mind grappled with questions. What had gone wrong with their plans? Wasn't Donald to meet him here last night? The terror of abandonment gripped him. Bewildered, he picked up his coat and draped it over his shoulders, walked to the nearby water cooler and gulped feverishly. Breakfast, he thought. Coffee with a roll dipped in it. Perhaps a cut of soft cheese. He looked around hesitantly.

A stewardess passed by and stopped. "Can I help you?"

"Thank you. I'm waiting for my son. He's a little late."

"Does he know your flight number and arrival?"

"Oh yes, thank you."

She smiled the official smile of all airline personnel, and walked on.

Father moved to the end of the waiting room and peered down the long promenade. There would be a coffee place in that direction. He rubbed his glass eye; it had developed an infection the past week which called for daily application of an antibiotic ointment, but that was in the stolen valise. He walked for what seemed a long distance and arrived at last in a complex of stores; they were not the same as he had seen the night before, or perhaps he'd forgotten. He stopped before a window with a menu posted on it, and entered. On the stool, he ordered oatmeal, coffee and a roll. How marvelous the food tasted! Especially the roll which, softened by the coffee, easily slid down his throat. Refreshed, he reached for his wallet. It was gone. He sat for a minute, stunned, trying to figure out what had happened. Carefully he went through all of his pockets, they were empty, except for a small penknife and a dime. While he slept, yes, during the night . . . he did recall being pushed . . . too drowsy to notice. Two boys ran off, he yelled at them, now he remembered!

He waited until the line at the cashier had thinned out, then approached the man at the register. "Excuse me, sir."

"Yes?"

"I had an accident, you see last night . . ."

"Where's your check?" The eyes were hard.

Father held out his check. "I hope you believe me, but last night, what happened—"

"Dollar sixty-five, Pop."

"If I can explain, I would appreciate . . ." His voice choked.

"You ain't got the money?"

171

Father stood still, humiliated, frightened. "I have a dime. But my son is supposed to meet me, he'll pay you . . ."

"Listen, guys like you floating around, you shouldn't come in if you haven't got the money, understand? This isn't a handout place. You want me to call a cop? Forget the dime. Just stay away." He took the check from the outstretched hand and turned to the man next in line.

Outside, into the promenade, Father drifted in the direction of the heaviest traffic, then wandered off into the concourse until stopped by the security guard, then back into the waiting room. It struck him that it wasn't the same waiting room where his flight had ended; the counters seemed the same, so did the chairs, and the arrival-departure screens overhead, yet he sensed a vague difference. Perhaps he was mistaken, all the waiting rooms were the same. This experience, as he wandered from one airline waiting room to another, utterly demoralized him. The hours went by, he drank water, he rested, he slept, then rose again, down another escalator, watching the baggage unload, up the escalator and into a new area. He lost all track of place. His energy low, he finally sat on the edge of a huge potted plant. What was his wife doing now? He wished he was with her, to help with her bath. Fran didn't know enough about it. It was a mistake not to stay together; he shouldn't have listened to her.

"Excuse me, sir." It was that nice lady in the blue uniform who had spoken to him earlier—was it the same day? "How are you getting on?"

His face took on a shy smile. "I spoke to you this morning, didn't I?"

"That's right. No luck yet, I see."

"I don't know . . ." he rose unsteadily.

"I mean your son, he was coming to pick you up." She

was studying him quietly, professionally. "That was yesterday, last night to be exact."

"Yes. He's coming. He'll be here."

"Are you sure you're not in trouble? Will you need a place to sleep tonight?"

He had not thought of the oncoming night, the subject had seemed too distant and unreal. "Oh no, he'll be here before night, no doubt about it. I appreciate your kindness." What a lovely remarkable girl, he thought.

"If you need help, please tell me," she said. "I mean, perhaps I can give you a lift in my car. I'm going into the city." She held out her hand.

His heart leaped. "Well, yes, if you're going that way . . . Is it downtown? Do you know where the post office is? If you can let me off at the post office, I can get home from there all right."

"Post office? I don't think I'm sure where—"

"Where the palm trees are. There's a little square with palm trees and a bench. I live very near that place, two streets away, I forget the name but I can get there if you'd be so kind as to drop me."

He saw something strange in the lady's face, a tremor of concern. She doesn't believe me, he thought. She doesn't know there are trees, just as I explained it.

She patted his arm. "Let me tell you what I can do for you, sir. You seem like an intelligent person, but you have a problem and need help. You can't sleep on the bench another night, can you?"

"If you would just drop me off at the post office—"

"You stay right here. I'll have a woman come by in a few minutes from our social service bureau who will help you." She spoke with assurance and gentleness. "She'll help you find your son, and find a place for the night if necessary.

173

Wait right here." She smiled and walked briskly away, lost in the corridors.

An instinct of danger reached a nerve in his mind. The lady was too sweet, and also peculiar. First, she offered him a ride, then she spoke of sending someone else to help him. He didn't like that. They meant to take him somewhere, and when Donald came and didn't find him here, he'd be very angry. No, he had to stay and wait. Huddling in his thin coat, he slinked off, through the revolving door, down an escalator, out another door, then down a walkway to another door which startled him by opening as his foot touched the rubber matting. He was in the lobby of a different airline, and drew a relieved breath. That nice lady was planning to take him somewhere . . . to a hospital? The idea sent a chill through him. She would never find him here, it was too big, each part looked the same and yet it was different. He shook his head in wonderment. A momentary feeling of safety soothed him.

Noticing a set of phones against the wall, he decided to use the remaining dime to call Donald. He tried to recall the number written down in his lost wallet. It began with 668, but was the rest 8434, or 8344, or possibly 4384? He tried very hard to concentrate on the individual numbers; after half a minute they floated around in his head like letters in an alphabet soup. He dialed information and was given a number, but when he dialed it something went wrong and he lost the dime. He explained this to the operator who switched him to another operator who asked his name and address for a refund. He said he needed the money now, and the operator told him to hold on and she would connect him to a supervisor. Then he heard a new voice that kept saying over and over again *Your phone requires a coin to complete this call your phone requires a coin* . . . He hung up, baffled. Should he ask the nice lady for another coin? He decided against that. It was safer not to ask anybody.

He felt Donald would turn up; he had to. After all, Fran had sent the letter, and even if the letter got lost they would have to meet and come for him. They knew he was here. A stubborn voice inside him argued that he must stay at the airport. He had to watch out for that nice lady who was planning to trick him somehow. If they caught him, he would not say anything, not even tell his name. He nodded grimly, he would be resolute. This idea pleased him, awoke some sleeping strength within him.

He was getting hungry again. Why not beg for coins? He had often seen old people beg. His appearance—the one good eye—would bring in the coins, he felt certain. Of course, he would never tell Fran or Donald about this. He'd wait a little while, and later, if he had the courage . . . No, he could never do that, he'd starve first.

By now, he had gotten the general layout of the airport in his head and he hurried toward the farthest wing. Donald would locate him through the paging system which he had observed in operation. Meanwhile, he would prove that he could cope with an emergency; this would show he was not too old for the farm; his son would be pleased with how he behaved. An escalator loomed up ahead. And then—was it possible?—he saw Donald. Yes, near the top of the escalator. He blinked, rubbed his eye, and looked again. The moving figure was almost at the swinging door. He called out, "Donald?" The figure vanished throught the door. "Is that you, son?" and he moved ahead more rapidly, stumbled on toward the ascending belt of stairs. His heart pounded. With an agility that surprised even himself, Father met the rising step that lifted him to the top and out of the door.

24.

She had driven all through the morning and into the afternoon, stopping only for coffee and a quick sandwich. She was in the final hours of her journey. The terrain widened out, spotted now with sprawl of trees and forest, the rise and fall of hills, scattered farms. Here the landscape of childhood formed again, and Fran rushed toward it with her soul unweighted, close to joy.

Sighting a gas station, she drove in. She would phone Donald to make sure everything was in order; she would have called him earlier, but too much was happening, he'd understand that. Did she say in her letter that she would call him on the day they were all to meet at the farm? She wasn't sure; he might be expecting to hear from her. She placed the call at the roadside booth, listened to the ring, and heard the receiver lifted.

"Hello?"

"Donald?"

"Yes."

"It's Fran. You sound breathless. Were you running?"

"Matter of fact, I was, just skipped up the stairs which I shouldn't be doing at my age." A silence. "Hello?"

"I'm here."

"Where are you?" She was annoying him again with those pauses.

"You'd never guess. I'm two hours away from the farm. The old farm, remember? I drove up in less than two days. I'm expecting all of us to meet there by end of the afternoon, which I explained in my letter to you."

"What letter?"

"Don't tell me you weren't surprised when they both got off the plane together! I wish I could have been there to see your face. Weren't they a sweet couple, Momma in that funny old hat with the cherries, and Poppa in his Army coat from God knows what war? They're like an old photograph in a family album."

"Where the hell are you?"

"Please don't shout, Donald."

"Where are you? Hello!"

She looked through the glass booth at the empty field in sudden panic. "I can't hear you."

"Are they with you? Did you bring the folks along with you?" Her strong breathing alarmed him.

"Now you stop that, Donnie. This is no time to joke. Make sure Momma takes along an extra sweater. It can get chilly up in the hills."

"There's nothing at the farm. It all burned down forty years ago when we were kids. There's only a foundation. Now would you explain . . ."

She swayed against the door of the booth. "Don't spoil it, please." Her hand gripped the top of the phone for support. "You're trying to spoil my plans. You're a bastard. If you don't show up with them, I'm going to call the police. Are you listening to me? You agreed. We discussed it a week ago, and you agreed it was the best plan. We couldn't just let them rot among strangers, they're our parents. At least they can die in a familiar place. Now Donald, you're teasing me, and I've had a long drive, so I'm going to hang up. You remember the road, don't you? Come the longer way, up Columbia Hill where Poppa used to drive his Model-T, he'll jump with joy at the sight." She could say no more, overcome with emotion. She dropped the phone and rushed out. "He'll be there, I know. He'll bring them," she said fiercely.

Donald's first thought was to get the operator and trace the call; instead he tried to decipher the message. It was either too clear or a garbled daydream. She could be anywhere, he shuddered, home or right around the corner; he recalled her tension and laconic behavior at their parting. Where was Rocky? As for the parents, why did she insist he bring them? He hurriedly dialed the landlord of their apartment who informed him that they had moved out two days ago.

"Moved out . . . where?" asked Donald, his anxiety rising.

"Out," was the reply.

"Who took them, please, Mr. Alberg."

"Who? Where? What? I don't see everything. Your father I think went on an airplane. Next day, your sister and mother drove away. How should I know where?"

"You said they drove away, together?"

"All I know, she told me the day before that she was going to pick up her mother."

"Did they give up the apartment?"

"I don't know. The rent is paid all month so I don't ask, it's not my business."

"Thank you." He placed the receiver down with a

178

feeling of dread. She was expecting him then. Was she alone? What the hell happened, he wondered, as he hurried to his car. The old man on an airplane . . . This was too elaborate, or too mad, to be a game. Why did she instruct him to bring them both to the farm? Her ghost of a farm. Knowing very well they could not possibly . . .

There was no other way but to meet her. As he hurried to his car, he tried to reconstruct the phone conversation. Underneath her rambling words he sensed disaster.

She was moving past the meadows now, barely two miles from her destination. The road from Blairstown joined at the intersection, and she made the turn south. Past the little red schoolhouse (no longer red), past the dairy (was that old Mr. Mayer waving from the field?), and the series of curves (oh that remembered shiver of joy when the Model-T swung from side to side), then the long downward grade (the same field of wildflowers), past the pumphouse (silent now), and ahead her breath held at the sight of the apple orchard in bloom. As the car approached the actual site—bare except for the foundation of the main building—her eye constructed another house she planned for them all: it flashed in the field and was gone.

She parked at the side of the narrow road, silent for many moments, her eyes closed, listening to the birdcalls through the open car window. The field beckoned like a voice; she left the car and walked toward it. As she moved, she thought of a Bergman movie long ago, it took place in the countryside; it had something to do with God, the heroine found peace that way. Now, here, under the bright open sky, Fran knew this was peace. Nothing was going to spoil it. If Momma ever yelled at her again, she would drown her in the well. Poppa would be too busy with his hammer and nails to bother anyone. If Donald refused to cooperate, she would have him arrested at once.

The ground dipped slightly near the exposed foundation where the original house stood in the years of their childhood. It had burned down. Uncle Victor probably did it, or Donald out of spite. Because of the fire, they had moved to the city where everything began to go wrong, her whole life. But there would be time now, years and years of it, for happiness. She was at the foundation, her eyes staring down into what was once the cellar. She could see the outline of the vanished kitchen and living room and bedrooms: it was like a cutout pattern for children. Descending the shaky stone steps that remained, she reached the dirt floor, grass and weeds covering some concrete slabs still intact, cluttered with old farming implements—a rusting hayrake, a plow, a variety of spades, rotting leather harness. She kicked a sharp object: a bent soup spoon! At her feet, half-hidden in the earth, were plates and cups, knives and forks; some dishes were broken and blackened, but enough remained for a serving, if one decided to have a picnic. Her excitement made her weak, forcing her to sit for a moment.

Fran picked up a cup and saucer, paired and miraculously white, and ran her hand across the crimson border of roses. It gave her fingers a tiny shock. Next, she found some spoons which glistened after a brisk rubbing with her handkerchief. She smiled and clapped her hands. It was all coming alive. She inhaled giddily.

From above, Donald observed her for a full minute before calling her name softly. She turned, still seated, and looked up at him. "Donald, did you see the blossoms in the orchard? Just behind you."

He didn't move. "Where are they, Fran?"

"Who?"

"Momma and Poppa."

She laughed warily. "Well, I certainly hope they're in your car. Go and fetch them, Donald. I have some cold cuts and bread and pickles. We can have a little picnic. Bring them please."

"Answer me. You put Poppa on a plane. When? To where? And you took Momma along with you on the trip. Where are they, for God's sake!"

She stood up, holding a spoon. "Are you going to spoil the picnic? Are you going to be a bastard to the very end?" She spoke calmly, matter-of-factly, not a trace of emotion. "You can bring the seat cushions from my car. Momma should not sit on the ground at her age. Poppa can sit on the stone step, he's like that, or he can stand. And you, brother, can help with the sandwiches. Now go on, they must be tired after the trip. Go and bring them." Her last sentence was a command with a touch of entreaty.

Donald had not moved. He feared saying the wrong word. She seemed poised on an abyss and the slightest tremor could send her toppling. He would get the cushions to stall for time. "Yes," he said. "You wait here."

His figure vanished from her sight. Then a deep psychic alarm sounded in her, she dropped the spoon and scrambled up the opposite side of the embankment. Without looking anywhere, she hurried—almost a runner's pace—toward the woods some five hundred yards distant. At the heavy grass bordering the woods, she walked firmly into the foliage and was lost in the dusk of the interior forest. The sun filtered dimly through the high maples and spruce. She was in the forest of her dream. She recognized it at once: the stillness, the opaque light, and her own presence both within it and as observer. Absent was the fear. Fear seemed to have been a garment she had dropped at the edge of the wood. Now her heart quickened at the thought of the dam. She determined to find it this time. She wanted to be able to tell Poppa exactly where it was, how pleased he'd be! She stopped, not sure which direction to take.

Just then she heard a voice calling distantly: "Fran! Frances! Where are you?" It was Donald. Well, let him call, she didn't intend to answer.

"Fran–cie! Do you hear me? It's Donald." His voice was muffled by the screen of trees.

"Of course it's you, Donald," she said aloud. "I know it's you. But I won't tell you where I am. You'll have to find me. All of you . . ."

"Helloa! Fran, can you hear me?"

She turned and plunged deeper into the forest until his voice, growing fainter, was lost altogether.

25.

"Y**ou** would not believe such a place. People running around, noise, and full of crooks. They stole my wallet, remember!"

"Yes, but you did get back home."

"And he never showed up. That son of mine never met the plane, what else to believe? Is he crazy, I wonder?"

Mother sighed as she took a sip of fruit juice. "It's Fran I'm worried about. Imagine, leaving me in the motel—"

"What motel?"

"The trip north, silly, to the farm, except we never got there. It was last week, don't tell me you forgot. She said goodnight to me, and when I woke up she was gone. Gone without a word. I could have died, didn't she realize that?"

"Well, you didn't die."

"No, and only because that nice motel man was kind enough to put me on a bus." She shook her head. "Not a single word from her. How do you explain that, dear? And I never got the chance to bathe in that pink bathtub. Where did she go, I wonder?"

Father coughed impatiently. "To a friend, Donald said,

in California. She's a looney, that one. They're both strange. They come down here two or three times a year, I mean before she moved here for good, and make plans for us, tell us how to live, what to do and not to do, and poof they're on the plane. As if we need someone to tell us how to live!" He struck the table with his fist, making the bowl of oranges tremble.

"They mean well, of course. Fran is very devoted."

"So there I was, at the airport," Father jumped back to his adventure. "You wouldn't believe it, you can walk around for hours, for days, and no one would notice."

"I'm sure it was terrible," said Mother straightening the cord of her hearing aid.

"It was my second day, my shoes were pinching me, I had to sit down. I was hungry, my wallet gone. It looked like the end. I tried to think. I had to find enough money to get home. I'm sitting there, staring ahead, when suddenly the name of the bank, right there, in front of me . . . it was my bank! A branch of my bank at the airport. I went inside. I looked like I slept in the gutter. I said to the guard, 'this is my bank.' And he said, 'what do you want? Go away.' I spoke louder, 'Take me to the manager. I'm no bum, I have money in this bank, in another branch, and I want some of it to get back home.' "

Mother sat up, alert. "You didn't tell me that."

"I'm telling you now. I went into the bank, I wasn't afraid of them."

"They didn't throw you out?"

"Throw me out? 'I demand to see the manager,' I said."

"You said that, looking like a tramp?"

" 'I'm not a nobody, sir. I have my money in your bank, three thousand dollars.' "

Mother gasped. "So that's what it is!"

"Yes. I had to tell them."

184

"But you wouldn't tell me, you vile man! Three thousand dollars. Keeping it a secret all these years. Hiding it from me. For shame!"

Father ignored her. "They asked me questions. They made phone calls. Then I signed a slip and they gave me two hundred dollars on the spot."

She sulked for a moment. "What will you do with the money now.?"

"I'm not giving any of it away, and that's that!"

Mother sighed. "All right. If you want to die with it, go ahead. I won't say a word."

"Next, I'm on a plane, then the D Bus waiting at the airport, I get off at my favorite corner with the two palm trees. From there, I could find my way."

"And so you did," she murmured.

"I didn't have to ask anybody for help. And Fran thought I was helpless—both of them!" He grinned triumphantly. "But the truth is, you need me and I wanted to come home."

"Oh, you liar!" Mother declared coquettishly.

"Well, you do. I think you do."

"I did miss you, dear. Victor came by, but he was no help, for a brother. I can't stand the way he keeps whistling through his teeth."

"Your side of the family is spooky."

She looked at him admiringly. "Imagine, you went all the way up there and back on an airplane all by yourself." They sat for several minutes in silence.

Father rose and turned to her. "Would you like some tea?"

"That would be lovely. With a lump of sugar, please."

26.

It was her third letter in as many days, and Donald had yet to open one of them. They came, as usual, in spurts, followed by a silence that would last for a week or many weeks, or longer. Now they had begun again. He knew the contents generally; they varied little from letter to letter. Ever since she entered the institution, her mind was frozen around a single vision of the past.

He opened the new letter. "Dear Donnie, it was nice to hear from you, all the news and friendly gossip. I even got a note from my ex asking if I needed anything. I said no, I want nothing from him. He's outside the family, after all. Before I forget, Donnie, let me tell you again how much I like this place. The nurses and doctors are very cooperative, they never get angry and treat you as an equal. I've become friendly with one of the nurses. I hope you will meet her on your next visit. By the way, when you come again, please remember to bring those old photographs of the farm. There's one with the white porch going all around the house. And that one with the peddler's wagon, with the

186

horse, and the leather flaps that rolled down along the sides for everyone to see what there was to buy, the scissors, and sewing needles, and combs, and little pocket mirrors. I remember Momma bought one for me, and you once got a small penknife but I suppose you forgot all about it. Please don't skip your next visit, Donnie, because I do so look forward . . ."

Donald folded the letter and placed it back in the envelope without reading to the end. It was mid-morning, still early enough in the day to make the hundred-mile return trip and be home by dinner. Over a month had passed since his last visit. He didn't know why he felt impelled to keep going. At least for awhile, he thought. Who else was there? The parents were far away, involved in their own precarious yet casual lives. Victor was out of it, phoning once for the facts, and then never again. And Rocky, the possible savior, going his own way in sunland, playing the horses and dogs, and probably not giving Fran's absence more than an idle thought, if at all. Even Donald wished he could be oblivious to her demons, her peculiar suffering.

On the two-hour drive, his mind threw up shards of remembered words, her disconnected sentences, whose real meanings evaded him. *Someone to speak for me . . .* What did she want said? *I turned to you Donnie . . .* He despaired of putting these clues into a pattern, clues to unlock a mystery which would, if released, only increase an unresolved guilt. Round and round the sentences raced in his head, a mesmeric song tuned to the sound of the motor rushing him toward that place.

The building came into view. Donald saw its dark facade half a mile away, looking obscenely like a movie set. As the car approached he felt his own accelerating heartbeat, and a wild desire to drive past and pretend he had taken a

187

wrong turn off the highway. But when the curved entrance rose up ahead, he wheeled the car into the graveled approach and parked.

Then he was inside, past the visitor's identification desk, past the guard, and into the long corridor leading to the visiting area where the patients strolled and chatted with friends and relatives. It was an open ward; large windows faced out upon an acre of lawn and garden.

Halfway through the corridor he saw her. There was still some distance between them. She wore a simple blue housedress, with low-heeled shoes; a pale lipstick was her total makeup, her hair plainly tied back.

Then she saw him. A smile flickered across her face. She started toward him, slowly at first, weaving through the small groups, pushing a few gently aside. She raised an arm in a tentative gesture. He waved back at her. Now she was clear of people and moved down the corridor to meet him. Her walk quickened, became a run as she crossed the distance between them. Her figure seemed, for an instant, to freeze in his vision, a reminder of a life arrested and soundlessly calling. Her eyes filled with light—wide, inquiring, wounded eyes—and she rushed into his arms.

"Oh Donnie," she whispered, "I'm so glad you could come. I knew you would."

He felt her against him. Her arms tightened, and clung. It seemed to him as though some turn of fate, begun long ago and forgotten, had determined that he be here at this moment, caught and helpless. He realized that she would never let go of him, wherever she was, even, he sensed with a chill, in death.

"It's all right, Fran. Everything's all right. I'm here."